Horse of a Different Color

Horse of a Different Color

Stories

Howard Waldrop

Small Beer Press
Easthampton, MA

This is a work of fiction. All characters and events portrayed in this book are either fictitious or used fictitiously.

Small Beer Press
150 Pleasant Street #306
Easthampton, MA 01027
www.smallbeerpress.com
www.weightlessbooks.com
info@smallbeerpress.com

Distributed to the trade by Consortium.

Library of Congress Cataloging-in-Publication Data

Waldrop, Howard.
[Short stories. Selections]
Horse of a different color : stories / Howard Waldrop. -- First edition.
pages cm
Summary: "Howard Waldrop's stories are keys to the secret world of the stories behind the stories . . . or perhaps stories between the known stories. From "The Wolf-man of Alcatraz" to a horrifying Hansel and Gretel, from "The Bravest Girl I Ever Knew" to the Vancean richness of a "Frogskin Cap," this new collection is a wunderkammer of strangeness"-- Provided by publisher.
ISBN 978-1-61873-073-2 (hardback) -- ISBN 978-1-61873-074-9 (ebook)
I. Science fiction, American. I. Title.
PS3573.A4228A6 2013
813'.54--dc23

2013028910

First edition 1 2 3 4 5 6 7 8 9

Text set in Centaur.

Printed on 50# 30% PCR recycled Natures Natural paper by the Maple Press in York, PA.

Old Guys With Busted Gaskets

This collection is about evenly divided between stories I wrote before and after May 2008.

Before May 2008 I was the usual amiable zany buffoon you've been following through these collections for thirty-something years.

After May 2008 I'd had quintuple bypass (as a charity patient) and could no longer walk (possibly a bad reaction to the anaesthesia) and spent, first six months in physical rehab at a VA hospital in Temple, Texas, and then two months at my sister Mary and bro-in-law Danny's house in Nettleton, Mississippi.

Believe you me, I'd undergone a sea-change (on dry land).

The first thing I'd been told in the ambulance on the way to Seton Hospital in 2008 was 1) you obviously had a silent heart attack sometime in the past to be having a flash pulmonary edema *now* and 2) you're diabetic.

Well, in the course of things (over the six months I was being retrained to walk at the VA hospital) the eyes began to go (this will be important in the discourse later).

A word of fatherly advice: if you're going to spend any length of time in a hospital, check your dignity and free will at the door (along with your shivs and shanks). It'll save time.

Anyway, since then and in the last few years, I've had many eye surgeries (both laser and meatball), mostly on the right eye, and some more's coming up.

Needless to say, this time of incapacity was also the time of the greatest opportunities I'd been offered in my career. (It goes without saying.) EVERYBODY wanted something from me, for more money than usual. Some of them got them, and some had to be as disappointed as I was.

I'm still finishing *The Moone World* and *The Search for Tom Purdue,* short novels you'll see shortly (all things being equal), and other stories here and there, of which I have a great steaming pile of ones I want to do.

I'll fill you in, in greater or lesser detail, in the Afterwords to the individual stories.

You've been warned.

Your Pal,
Howard

Why Then Ile Fit You

One of the ones I can see told me it is already the year 1951. Good Gracious!

I believe one of the other ones told me it was 1950, last year, when they took me out to act in *David and Bathsheba.*

I can't keep them straight anymore, the years or the people floating in and out of here—they come, they go, the ones I can see and the ones no one can.

It had been good to see Hoey again on that quasiBiblical set—we had not acted together since he was Lestrade and I Moriarty—No, no, it was the *other* one, the one in Washington, where I wasn't Moriarty—how long ago was that? It must be years and years. The time goes by—I never know whether it has been a day, two minutes, or five years since something occurred.

They even tell me I was in a film two years ago—a musical with Gene Kelly and Judy Garland. I have absolutely no memory of that. Upon my soul, I do not.

You see, my agent comes to get me—I'm sure he has checked with the staff and doctors, and has probably even talked to me, but I do not remember that, either—and he takes me to the studios, and I act, and there are various pleasantries, and then I find myself back here in what I have come to refer to as Shady Bedlam Manors, though I am sure the name is something quainter, more reassuring. Others here call it The Home for Old and Bewildered Actors . . .

I have just noticed an insect—some beetle or one of the true bugs—which probably flew in when the wide back doors were open during visiting hours. It seems to like the very-well-designed bed-side lamp on the somnoe—it is crawling in an endless pattern over the rim of the shade, down inside, across the far side, reappearing at exactly the same place above the rim each time.

I shall time its circumnavigation of the lampshade. Perhaps this will give me a clue to . . . something or other.

Appropriately enough, my clock has stopped. I give a small laugh, and think that it has been a long time since I've done *that.*

Still the insect appears, disappears, reappears, so time does go on . . .

I must have been doing something naughty, or nonU, and been seen, for I find myself lightly restrained to my bed.

I must have told them about the insect, or it found its way out of the Magellanic voyaging of its Luciferian world, for now it is gone.

And I am reminded of poor Dwight Frye. How long now? There we were, in my fitter years, making *Dead Men Walk* in the middle of the war. I am playing, if I remember right, a vampire whose one goal in life is to suck all the blood out of his twin brother—also me—a

Goody Two-Shoes. And then there's Dwight, doing his usual, as Jewish-Americans say, schtick, giving it his all, like always. And then there he is, lying dead of a heart attack, at little more than half my age.

How many deformed and demented human wrecks did he play in his time? Twenty? Thirty? In the movies, and more on stage. The fellow was a fine actor. Yet there we both were on Poverty Row, bugging our eyes out like Mantan Moreland . . .

It was as nothing that each of us had Shakespeare, Shaw, Galsworthy in our pasts, great and enduring roles. There we were in films which barely lasted as long in theaters as it takes to dress for dinner at a country house weekend . . .

And now, Dwight dead and me here.

Someone I couldn't see must have been here. My restraints are gone. There is a new clock on the bedside table. It seems to be working very well.

There is also a swelling in my left arm—a sure sign one I can't see has given me an injection, while the others are invisibly ransacking my room, looking for money or sweets. Or watching me. Jove knows what.

One can never be sure whether they are there or not.

I often wonder if it were for my eyes that I was cast as all those crazy doctors, Moriarty, small-town Torquemadas. It was a small trick—letting the face go soft but keeping the eyes hard, flinty, moist. An old Victorian rep thing—I learned it from older heavies and villains when I was playing leads in my much younger days. Then came the films, and I worked in them. And one reviewer had said: "He enters the movie. His eyeballs come on the screen before the rest of his head does."

I *never* forgot that review.

I had a very nice letter from dear old Jimmie Whale yesterday. He says he will come out of retirement—what, ten, twelve years now? —and direct a film again, but only if I appear in it.

I call my agent. Then I am asking one of the male nurses if he thinks I am well enough to do a movie again, when one of the invisible ones comes in, makes me do a bad thing, I think, and then jabs me in the arm with the kind of needle they always had me fooling with at Monogram and PRC, the kind that is really used to extract blood from cattle and horses for serum . . .

This morning, free of the bands again, I write Jimmie a courteous note, thanking him for the offer but telling him I really don't feel up to it. I do not know if he is really trying to come out of his self-imposed exile only a few miles from here, or is just being kind to me, or if I am favoring him with a negative reply, that he expects, so he won't have to go through with all the bother and nonsense.

Out here, in what others call Tinseltown, one can never be sure who is doing a favor for whom.

I just don't want to embarrass myself, or Jimmie, if there were a movie and I were in it.

Dear old Marjorie Main. Now playing Ma—what? Some utensil. Ladle? Pot? Kettle—yes, Kettle! She could always out act almost anyone she was onscreen with. Now that she has the security of a series, she can pick and choose her other roles, and can perhaps slow down.

Dear Eve Arden. I can now listen to her on the radio, in the teacher part, Constance Brooks.

Dear old—Ah! What's the use. If I keep going on like this I shall begin to sound like Dear Old Boris Karloff. One thing is sure—he and Lugosi will be doing this stuff forever, dropping in harness like Dwight. Only, fittingly and not nearly so young . . .

I must have been asleep in my chair, in my dressing gown, reading Cedric Hardwicke's book.

There was a touch on my arm.

I opened my eyes. "George," he said.

"Jimmie!" I said, dropping the book to the floor, reaching for it.

He retrieved it, putting it on my reading table, carefully placing the bookmark in it before closing it.

Except for a few wrinkle lines, and the fact that his hair was now pure white, he hadn't changed a bit in more than a decade. (I've not had more than a fringe of hair at the back of my head since my late thirties . . .)

"Jimmie, old fellow! What brings you here?"

"Well, George," he said, "the movie might be on again, and I've come to ask you once more to be in it. I absolutely won't, can't do it without you."

"It's very nice of you to ask, Jimmie, but—look about you. Does this seem to be the lodging of a *working* actor? Scripts everywhere, bad food boiling in a pot, unpaid bills stacked up? No. This is very much the room of an *ex*-actor."

"You know as well as I, George, that it's like the sound of the bell to an old firehorse out to pasture—the right role comes along, you can smell it like a fire, miles away. I'm surprised you hadn't written me in the last few weeks, scenting the script."

"Of course, that's the line *every* producer or director uses on *every* old bunged-up actor," I said. "I believe I heard Beerbohm Tree used it on Mrs. Patrick Campbell herself, a couple of years before he *himself* quit producing and started teaching."

"No, George. This time it's a real role. I promise you, you won't have to eat a rat, or anything. You get to act. An actor's dream!"

"But not, I'm sure, alas, *actor-proof*," I said.

"At least tell me you'll look at the script if I send it," he said, smiling earnestly. "When I first asked you, two years ago, it wasn't quite ready. Now it is."

"Oh, Jimmie. I'm truly flattered. But I'm so rusty."

Jimmie put his hand on my shoulder. "I absolutely can't do this without you, George. It will be bad enough coming back to *all that.* I really don't want to do this if you don't."

"Oh, Jimmie," I said. I believed him. "Ask Karloff. I don't think he's taken a day off since 1931, and that was a world away. You and he did so well together, every time out . . ."

"Karloff isn't right for the part, George," he said quietly. "No matter how well he and I got on and helped each other, he would have to tie himself in a knot—no doubt he'd find some way to do it—but why do that, when it's your role in the first place? Something you can do as naturally as . . . as reading Sir Cedric's book there?"

"I'm just too old and too . . . too confused to do a film just now. You're seeing me at my best, my very best. I haven't felt so good in, oh, days and days. And those, Jimmie, are becoming more and more infrequently. Good days, I mean."

He laughed. "I believe you're having Fear of Success, George."

That broke much of the tension. I called down for tea to be brought up. (Wrong time of day, I know: Jimmie used to have real tea at four on his sets for all the expatriate Brits—Karloff, Lanchester, himself, anyone else vaguely British or colonial—and there were lots of us in the old days.)

We talked, then, about those old days and compatriots. He caught me up on such gossip as he had; after a while I showed him around the place, feeling quite the squire. He paused in the walk to talk with another old, old actor, who'd been in *Journey's End* when Jimmie had come over to direct it in New York before coming out here to film it in 1930. It was very nice of Jimmie to do that; the man was much older than I and had been in this place long before I got here.

Before he left, Jimmie, of course, asked me to reconsider one more time, and I of course declined.

That night I had a dream. In the dream, I was asleep. People kept waking me up and giving me Academy Awards. I kept telling them to get out and let me sleep. Every time I got back to sleep, another person came in and gave me another one. I had more than Walter Brennan, more than some scene designers, more than costumers, more than anyone. And all I really wanted was sleep.

When I awoke in the morning, I was surprised to find that the room wasn't full of gold statuettes. Same old room; same bedside stand, same chairs and tables. No Academy Awards.

I was out of sorts all that day and the next.

The only trouble with this place, fine though it is, is that they think I'm crazy. Don't they know it's not me, but the ones *I* can't see, *they* can't see, that are doing things to me? I don't know if they—the Unkind Ones—are truly invisible, or whether they just move so fast the human eye cannot take them in. I have suggested to the doctors they set up some—is it undercranked or overcranked?—time-lapse cameras to test this latter hypothesis.

I have been reading a book of famous last lines, dying words of the famous, notorious, and not-so-either. Such as that of the condemned man who stepped onto a rickety scaffold and asked the sheriff "Is it safe?" Or the last words of Arthur Flegenheimer, that is, Dutch Schultz, which was more than four thousand words long spoken in a raving 104° delirium, which ended with the words "French Canadian Bean Soup."

I shall try to exercise enough restraint that my last ones should not be something like "bibblebibblebibble . . ."

One of the new nurses, named I think Bettina, brought my paper in this morning.

"Mr. Zucco," she said. "They asked me to tell you that Mr. Whale passed away yesterday."

I could tell that she was upset. I reached out and patted her hand.

"There, there," I said. "I'm sure it was time for him to go, and I'm sure it was for the best."

She left. Whale. Whale? Where have I heard that name before? Possibly an old, *old* timer.

I shall have to ask Jimmie next time I see him if he knew anyone named Whale. Strange name, that.

One of the Unkind Ones is here: but this one I can *see.* It is not one of the people I can usually see—but I know that she is one of the ones usually invisible. She looks somewhat like Aquanetta from the Paula the Ape Woman movies. (If it were her, I could make her laugh. I could do that, like I used to do, with the woman who played Pauline Dupree, by simply saying; "Rondo Hatton: Why the long face?")

But it is not her. I know, because she has with her the longest, largest hypodermic syringe imaginable. It is grotesquely huge. In her other hand is a cotton swab, smelling of alcohol.

Inside the glass barrel of the syringe is a green liquid filled with dancing, moving sparks of light. She is not here to take, but to give.

She leans close. Her breath is sweet.

"The Russians," she says warmly, tenderly, "have put up a satellite."

She swabs my bared arm.

"It's called the *Sputnik,*" she says, and plunges the giant needle in.

This must be something akin to what a heroin or cocaine or opium addict feels—this sense of bliss and happiness, well-being and, and—of knowing and understanding Everything!

It was like those movies I was in—all the potions, the brain-and-spinal-fluids, the suspended-animation gasses they always had me mucking about with!

Of course! Of course I see it all now. So sharp and clear! The needle is just a metaphor for the transcendent power of

Afterword
Why Then Ile Fit You

I've written about a lot of real people in my stories, from Karloff and Presley in "Ike at the Mike" to Peter Lorre in "The Effects of Alienation." You do research, you put them in stories where only they fit. (As I tell people, I wrote "The Effects of Alienation" to see what effect Hitler winning WWII would have had on Peter Lorre. Lots.)

But George Zucco is sort of a forgotten bogeyman of horror film. A classically trained actor, he appeared in many Universal (and Monogram and PRC) films alongside Bela Lugosi.

At the same time, he was a respected character actor in big-budget A movies from MGM and Twentieth Century-Fox (*Hunchback of Notre Dame* (1939) for one, and as Moriarty in some Rathbone Sherlock Holmes movies).

He was always better than any piece of crap he happened to be in; he never gave that idea, or not gave it the best the script allowed him.

Directors tried to get him out of his early retirement (in his sixties), and he evidently suffered from some mental difficulties.

I tried to get this stuff across in the story.

This appeared in *The Silver Gryphon,* the 25th publication of Golden Gryphon Press. Now, the late Press. They had a great run, publishing some fine upscale books (and me), including George Zebrowski's *Black Pockets* and *Empties* and a ton of others. They'll be missed.

The Wolf-man of Alcatraz

"Madame, I regret to say that we of the Bureau are unable to act in cases of lycanthropy, unless they have in some way interfered with interstate commerce."

—J. Edgar Hoover, 1933

When something loped across the moonlit bridge, the truckdriver slammed on his brakes and swung to the left, taking out three Tri-State Authority tollbooths.

Early one afternoon, they came to take him from his cell in D Block, down to the solitary vault built for him.

"Oh," said Smitty from the next cell, "that time of the month, huh?"

"Yeah, well," said the prisoner. He picked up a couple of the astronomy books from his bunkside shelf.

"Uh, warden says we'll have to get everything out of the place before dark this time, Howlin," said Sawyer, sergeant of the guards. "Losing too much prison issue. And books."

"Sorry," said Howlin. "I just have to check a few things. Be through before evening."

"That's okay, then," said Sawyer.

As he passed Smitty's cell, he looked at the big calendar on Smitty's wall, the one marked over with a big X each day, with the lunar phases in the empty squares along the bottom.

"See you—Tuesday, Smitty."

"Sure thing, Bob. Try to get some shut-eye."

"Always *try,*" said Howlin, from down the block.

They took him down from the cells and up the enclosed spiral staircase turrets of the gun gallery with their ports that gave clear fields of fire to every part of the cell blocks and corridors. They crossed down under the maximum-security floor, then went down the freight elevator, out of it, and down another corridor. There was another stairwell at the end that led to the part of the prison under the old military fort.

The hall was like that of the solitary block, but the walls were of smooth-finished concrete, forty feet long. Only two doors interrupted it. A guard opened his cell with a key and a combination lock. The cell had a Diebold vault door, twelve inches thick, with a total rim lock of interleaved 1-inch chrome-steel wafers. It could have held King Kong.

"Doc'll be here to see you around four o'clock, see if there's anything you want," said Sawyer. "I'll pick up everything but the blanket then."

"Sure thing, Sergeant," said Howlin.

Sawyer turned and went out. The door swung to behind him; he heard the rim-wafers slam down like teeth.

"You want your shot now?" asked the old doc.

"I guess so," said Howlin. "Could you make it a little stronger than last time? I think I remembered *something.*"

"I can't give you anything much stronger, Bob," said the doc. "We don't want you becoming an addict." He smiled a quick smile.

He readied the hypodermic. "All I can promise you is, I give you this now, it should keep you out for at least four hours. Depending. Sunset—"

"Sunset's at 5:43 PST; moonrise at 5:45," said Howlin. "*That* I know."

"So you should be out a couple of hours afterwards. By the way, a couple of medical types would like to examine you . . ."

"When's my next physical?"

"Next month, I think. I'll check."

"If they do it then, I don't mind. They meat docs or head docs?"

"One each."

"Long as I don't have to do a lot of foolishness, like when I first got here."

"You ready?"

He rolled up his prison uniform sleeve. "Shoot," he said.

The doctor put the needle in. With a sigh, Howlin leaned back on the single blanket on the concrete bunk and put his hands behind his head.

Sergeant Sawyer picked the books up from the floor, stepping around the water bucket and the slop jar.

"Thanks, Doc, Sergeant," said Howlin. Then his eyes closed, and his chest rose and fell slowly.

Sawyer and the doctor went out into the corridor. The guard closed the vault door like it was the end of a business day at a bank.

The sergeant went back up into the guardroom in the gallery overlooking the hallway and put the books in a small shelf there.

The doc followed, and a guard let him out into the stairwell that led back to the elevator.

A little past five, two guards reported to the night sergeant. He went to an armory cabinet, took out two Thompson submachine guns, handed one to each guard. Then he unlocked another cabinet, took out two thirty-round circular magazines marked LYC in silver paint on each drum and handed them to the guards. They slid the bolts back, slipped the drums in the receivers, and let the bolts go forward: one, two.

One of the guards was let out into the hallway and stood near a chair they put there, ten feet from the vault door.

The other one opened the gun port directly across from the door in the gallery and put the barrel of the Thompson through it.

They were attentive till the night sergeant left, then relaxed. The one in the hallway sat down.

"Pretty much like watching paint dry, isn't it?" asked the one in the gallery, a newer guard.

"In many ways," said the one in the chair.

"Does anything ever *happen?*" asked the new man.

"Plenty *happens,* I understand," said the guy in the hall. "Nothing so far that affects anybody out *here.*"

A couple of hours later the two guards thought they began hearing noises through the twelve inches of steel door. The hair on the new guard in the gallery stood straight up under his cap. He knew he would have to listen to eight more hours of this.

No wonder there was a 30 percent turnover in the guard staff on The Rock, he thought.

"Poor bastard," said the guy down in the corridor. Then he lit a cigarette.

March 4, 1937
Box 1476
Alcatraz, California
Prof. M. H. Nicolson
Smith College

Dear Professor Nicolson:
I have just finished your article on early Moon voyages in the new *Smith College Studies in English.* I would like to suggest a line of research for you (since you seem to be ideally suited for it)—for what reason were there so many plays dealing with the Moon (and other planets) in the late 1600s and early 1700s in England—Aphra Behn's *Emperor of the Moon*—which I think had its base in an Italian or French farce—of 1687; Thomas D'Urfey's *Wonders in the Sun* (1706), Elkanah Settle's *The World in the Moon* of 1697? Was it just, as you imply, a reaction to the new worlds revealed in the telescope and microscope, to a world also undergoing violent changes in religion? Or just exuberance at the reopening of the theaters, the Restoration and the Glorious Revolution?

And why should the figure of Domingo Gonsales, The Speedy Messenger, figure in *so* many of them, with his framework raft pulled by swans to the Moon, where they overwinter? Surely it can't be because Bishop Godwin was an Englishman—the first edition was published anonymously, and most people—because of Domingo's name and the fictitious biography—took it to be a translation from the Spanish or French?

And why "Speedy Messenger"? Was this Godwin's sly reference to Galileo's Starry Messenger?

I'm sure you, too, have thought about some of these things, but that they weren't in the scope of your article. Perhaps you're planning more work of this nature, or know of where I can find other articles of this kind? I would appreciate knowing of any forthcoming works on the same subject.

I have to admit I came across your article quite by chance—the *Smith College Studies* was meant for someone else here and was delivered to me by mistake. But it has been a revelation to me, and I want to thank you.

Sincerely,
Robert Howlin
#1579

"I don't know, Doc," he said to the visiting psychiatrist. "I don't remember *anything.* I wake up weak as a kitten. The first morning's the worst, because I know it's going to happen two more times before I'm through with it for the month."

Dr. Fibidjian looked down at the thick bundle of papers in the file.

"And you still don't know how it happened?"

"Like it probably says somewhere there. I was in a clip joint. A fight broke out. Somebody used a chair on the lights; somebody else took out the bartender, who I had been talking to, with a bottle. I was pretty busy there in the dark for a few minutes—I think I gave as good as I got. When it was over, there was a couple of big bites out of my left arm. A friend put some caustic balsam on it, and it was fine. Then, come the next full moon, I *was* like I *am.*"

"Do you think you belong in a mental institution, rather than here? That your condition is medical, rather than criminal?"

"I don't think there's a mental institution that could hold me—look what it says about Atlanta there," he said. "Besides, they tell me I killed four people—aside from the turnpike thing, I mean."

"Do you remember the circumstances of—"

"I told you, I don't remember *anything*, ever, Doc." He took a drink of water from the glass by the pitcher on the table of the conference room.

"Would you like a smoke?" asked Fibidjian.

"I don't smoke, Doc," he said. "I trade mine for books. I've got the book privileges for half the cons in this joint for the next five years. I chew gum, though. Beeman's Black Jack."

"Sorry," said the psychiatrist. "I'm fresh out."

"I've got the supply of *that* tied up, too," said Howlin.

The doctor looked over his notes.

"You say you have no memory of the murders of the three—"

"Postmen," Howlin said. "I seem to have a thing for postmen. What the two postmen were doing out, after dark, in the truck, in the summer, I don't know. But evidently they were. The wrong guys in the wrong place at the wrong time, I guess. Like the one the next night . . ."

"And the other?"

"They tell me it was a child." He shrugged. "As far as I know, it could have been Mussolini or Neville Chamberlain."

He looked at the psychiatrist. "The part that bothers me is there could be others they haven't found, people who just disappeared one moonlit night. I was bitten in May. I didn't cause that wreck 'til November. That's seven months. That seems a long time for only four people, doesn't it?"

"Uh, I agree," said the psychiatrist. "But the convictions were for the three postmen, and the turnpike accident. Those are the reasons you're *here*."

Howlin got up and whacked his hand against the thick concrete walls of the room. "The reason I'm *here,*" he said, "is that this is the only place on Earth that can *hold* me."

He rubbed the inside of his right elbow.

"Sore?"

"Your other doc friend has jabbed me somewhere every two hours since last night. He's running out of places to put the needle to draw blood."

"Maybe we should knock off awhile, then. I want to give you some simple tests this afternoon."

"All this is fine by me, Doc. You guys are earning me a dozen extra books this year."

"And that's what you want?"

"Look, Doc," he said. "I'm going to be here the rest of my life. Books are the only way I'll ever get to experience the outside, or see the world, or meet a woman or fish for bluegills in a pond. I can do all that in books. They're all I have except these walls, those bars, my cell, and the exercise yard."

"What if we can find *some* way to cure you?"

Howlin laughed.

"Doc, there is no cure for this but *death.* There's nothing you or I or anyone on this planet can do about that. Don't go dreaming there is."

Before the next full moon, they had installed, high up in the isolation vault, an 8mm camera, the lens of which was behind a small opening eleven feet up one wall, pointed toward the concrete bunk area.

The two doctors had turned it on at ten-minute intervals throughout the night from within the gun gallery where the second guard with the tommy gun stood.

Before they turned on the camera they turned on the single lightbulb in its reinforced metal cage, which was on the ceiling fifteen feet up.

When they went in with the prison doc the next morning, they found Howlin naked, his clothes and the bedding destroyed, his toes and fingernails bleeding. The prison doc gave him vitamin and painkiller shots, and he was in a deep sleep. They saw that some of the torn bedding had been stuffed into the hole hiding the camera lens, eleven feet up.

They retrieved the camera from its drilled-out space in the wall above the vault door. They took the prison boat over to San Francisco and had the film developed. They returned in six hours. From the boat they watched the ritual of the docking. The lieutenant in charge of the boat took the ignition key out and sent it—via a clothesline pulley—three hundred feet up the hill to the guard tower. It would not be sent down 'til the boat was ready for the return run and the lieutenant gave an "all okay" signal—which changed every day. They went from the boat directly to the warden's office, where the warden, prison doc, and captain and sergeant of the guards waited with a projector rigged to run on the island's DC electrical system.

They pulled the blinds, turned off the lights, and started it up.

Fibidjian read off his notes by the light as the leader went through. "First one should be 7:14 p.m., a couple of hours after sunset when the sedatives were wearing off."

The first scene leapt up. The cell was lit. Howlin wasn't on the bedding. There was a flash of movement, the move of a shadow at the lower edge of the frame.

Then something came up to cover the lens—the bedding strip. Then the screen went dark.

And stayed that way through the rest of the reel.

"That's *it?*" asked the captain of the guards. "Could we see it again, slower maybe?"

Fibidjian rewound the film, showed the scene over, frame by frame.

"Hold it," said the warden. "Right *there.*"

It was the bedding coming up. For three frames. At the edge of the cloth in the second frame was the outline of—was it a hand? Was it something else?

The next morning, while Howlin slept, they brought the workmen in. The camera had been destroyed, and the hole around the lens had been chipped away for two inches.

They reconcreted it with a piece of three-inch-in-diameter rebar inside, repoured, and never tried anything like the filming again.

November 29, 1939
Box 1476
Alcatraz, California
Professor E. C. Slipher
Lowell Observatory
Flagstaff, Arizona

Dear Professor Slipher:
I understand there are at present *no* plans to use the new 200-inch telescope at Mount Palomar for observations of the Moon. I understand that would be like using an elephant gun on a gnat.

I read in *Sky and Telescope* the field of view would be something like 2½ miles across viewed from 17 miles away, at least twice as good as any telescope used on the face of Luna before.

I believe this is a rare opportunity to look for the anomalies reported on the Moon in the last century—the signs of light in various areas, possible volcanic activity in the Sinuous Rille from 1879; the blue glow coming from differing areas, and the changes in craters Alphonsus, Hercules, and Eratosthenes.

It would be wonderful—and scientifically useful—if some small fraction of time—a night each month or two, perhaps just a few hours of that time—could be used for direct or photographic observation of these areas of the Moon.

Perhaps we can settle the question once and for all, of whether the Moon is a dead world, or is in some way *still* active, perhaps even with small traces of an atmosphere or the tenuous presence of water vapor deep within the craters—which, until man attempts to go there, can only be answered—*perhaps*—by using the best equipment available.

I'm sure time on the wonderful new telescope is heavily booked. But if you, like me, believe we should do this, I would hope you could broach the possibility at the next meeting of the American Planetary Society, and at the International Astronomical Union Satellite Section in March.

Thank you very much.

Sincerely,
Robert Howlin
#1579

———

The great WWII outside was a rumor. The guards got older for a while, or had small disabilities that could keep them out of the Army or Navy, but not out of the staff of Alcatraz.

The wind blew off the Bay as hard as ever; Angel Island still sat out there, the closest piece of land; San Francisco across the exercise yard looked the same, bright and white in good weather, grey and wet in bad; disappearing completely in the solid-wall fogs so thick you couldn't see the Industries Building from the boat dock.

The magazines and books came, the letters went. The days were the same as the years. They were marked only by his monthly trips outside the cell block and down to the old fortress area and the vault for three days of amnesia, weakness, and vertigo.

On the second of May, 1946, prisoners AZ 415 Coy and AZ 548 Kretzer, using a screw jack they'd built in Industries and smuggled in through the Laundry, got into the gun gallery and overpowered the only armed guard in the cell block. They got M-1 carbines and .45 automatics, and then surprised nine unarmed guards in the block one at a time, including the captain, who'd been wounded back in the big breakout attempt in 1938—and put them all in two cells at the end of D Block.

They opened cells and let others out.

The place was chaos a few minutes until the others realized they didn't have the keys that would get them out of the cell-block building.

One of the two instigators went berserk and started firing with a .45 auto into the cells full of guards, killing two of them and wounding all the others.

The youngest prisoner on The Rock went into the cells and told Coy and Kretzer, "They're *all* dead."

Five or six prisoners, including one named Hubbard, joined the two with the guns. Most of the rest returned to their cells. This had been just a short break in the routine.

Coy began firing out the windows, indiscriminately, at the rest of the Island.

The second day of the siege—with another guard dead on the hill outside, and marines from the Presidio, just back after 3½ years of kicking Tojo butt, were on the roof of the cell block, throwing tear gas and hand grenades down into the utility corridors that ran between each row of cells.

The warden had been on the horn for two days, urging the prisoners to give up.

Most inmates were hunkered in their cells, their heads down inside their bailed-out toilets, breathing fresh air from there, away from the tear gas that floated like ground fog through the building.

Word came up to Coy, Kretzer, and Hubbard, who were still firing at anything that moved outside.

"Howlin wants to talk with you."

"I'm *busy,*" said Coy, shooting toward the exercise yard.

"I think you better go talk to him."

"I *better,* huh?" said Coy, bringing the carbine around. He coughed, his eyes closed to slits. Snot hung down his chin in a rope.

"I'm just the messenger," said the inmate.

Machine gun bullets ricocheted off the walls above them, fired from the lower hill. What glass was left came down in an avalanche.

Coy went down to the other end of Broadway, where all the cell blocks junctioned.

Howlin sat calmly on his bunk, surrounded by his books, tears running down his swollen face. He wiped his face with a sock. He coughed quietly.

"Yeah?" said Coy.

"Have you been listening to the warden?" asked Howlin.

"It's the usual wind," said Coy.

"Those are Marines on the roof. They're sending Federal Marshals from as far away as Colorado."

"You ain't telling me nothing I don't know. I ain't afraid of Marines."

"I know you're not," said Howlin. "That's your choice. And I don't like being in here any more than you do. But it's not the Marines I'm worried about, either."

Hubbard and Kretzer joined them. "It's quiet," said Kretzer. "They'll yell if the soldiers try anything. What's up?"

"I don't know yet," said Coy. "Get to the point, Howlin."

"You don't have the keys to get out of the cell-block building. There's no other way out of here. They'll jackhammer their way in through the roof soon. There's three, maybe five of you with guns. There's hundreds of them. It's pretty much over."

"You *scared?*" asked Hubbard.

"Yes. But not—"

The sound of two prisoners having sex in a cell down the way came to them.

Coy jumped up and fired down Broadway. "You *animals* disgust me!" he yelled. He wiped his eyes and nose, coughed hard and couldn't stop.

"Coy," said Howlin. "Tonight is the full moon. If this isn't over before it comes up, and they haven't got me down to the isolation vault, you, and every prisoner here, will be locked in with *me.*"

Hubbard and Kretzer looked at Coy, then back at Howlin, sitting among his books.

"He's crazy!" said Hubbard.

"Maybe. Probably," said Howlin.

"Why don't we kill him *now?*" asked Kretzer.

"What's he done to us?" asked Hubbard. "He's stuck in here like us, crazy or not. He didn't break out."

Coy rubbed his eyes.

Howlin lifted his leg off the floor, cupped both hands around his knee. "I thought I would tell you what's *going* to happen tonight, since in your excitement you might have forgotten me. You can listen to me, or you can listen to the warden: I don't care. They've got their timetable for dealing with you—I have no idea what that is. I only know mine, and that I can't help myself, once it starts.

"If that happens, you might as well eat those guns now. They won't do you any good. The only ones that'll work on me are down there in the vault level, and you can't get *there,* either. Bars won't help; I'll come through them like they were butter. Not only that, I'll get everyone in the cell-block building, one at a time. Then I'll start in on the Marines when they get in, and the rest of the Island. Then I'll take the boat and do in San Francisco.

"You've got eleven hours and fourteen minutes. That's all I wanted to say."

There was more noise from up on the roof, and the three left.

Six hours later, they threw out the guns and surrendered. The Marines came in and secured the cell blocks. The guards took out the dead and wounded and set up fans to blow away the tear gas.

It was a few minutes 'til sundown when they got Howlin down to the isolation vault, and the doc in.

One day in 1953, the new prison doctor, who'd only been there six months, came into the cell vault on the morning after the first night of the full moon.

He found Howlin sitting up on the bedding of the concrete bunk.

The doc was taken aback.

"Are you okay?" he asked.

"*You* tell me, Doc. I'm jumpy as hell. But I *think* I stayed awake the whole night. I don't think anything happened. I could be wrong about that as about anything else—I could have only *imagined* I stayed awake. But I *think* I did."

The doc moved a flashlight beam across Howlin's eyes, then used the stethoscope.

"Let's assume you've been awake the whole night. I'll give you your vitamin shot, and a sedative. I'll be back this afternoon and give you another. Maybe you can sleep through the whole night for the first time in—what?—nineteen years?"

"What's happening to me, Doc?"

"I'm not a guessing man," said the doctor. "Until I know better, I would say you're getting *old*. There's some tests we can run next week."

Howlin looked down at the concrete floor. "Other than the great relief about it, I don't think I *like* the idea of getting old, Doc."

"Happens to the best of us," said the doctor, loading up the needle.

His book—*The Moon and Me*—came out October 6, 1957, two days after the Sputnik went up. He had gotten copies two weeks before but couldn't have any kind of celebration. He, and half the prison population, were down with the Asian Flu, brought back by one of the schoolkids on the boat.

Already they were talking of closing down The Rock. But then, they'd been talking about *that* since about two days after it opened in 1934.

"It doesn't look good," said the doctor. "If we'd caught it earlier, we could have operated. It's slow growing. It started in the gonads—I think now that must be why your condition went away. But now it's spread everywhere. You may have one or two years, or less. It's a tough break, Bob. I'm sorry as I can be."

"To think, Doc—the thing that's cured me's going to kill me. There's your irony."

"We're trying to get you transferred to the prison farm in Missouri," he said. "The medical board meets next week in Walla Walla."

"That would be great, Doc. You know what? If I do get there, I'm going to try to get permission to go out in the night and just *look* at the full moon. I haven't seen the Moon all these thirty years. I may see the Moon on the train, but it probably won't be full. Yeah, that would be *great,* Doc. I can last *that* long."

They made a movie about his life—*The Wolf-Man of Alcatraz*—which starred Kirk Douglas, who looked nothing like him, and which was highly fictionalized. Howlin never saw it.

—

They came up to the top of the hill, Howlin using one of those new prison farm–issue three-toed canes made of aluminum.

The hill looked like all of the other ones that stretched away toward Jefferson City over to the east.

The Moon sailed on the rim of the world like a big, bright ocean liner, or a giant pumpkin. It seemed so close you could touch it.

"Kids'll be trick-or-treating next week, won't they, Captain?" asked Howlin.

"Suppose so."

"Man, you shoulda seen the Moon in the old days. It was *really* somethin'."

The captain shrugged.

"People are going there someday. I can feel it."

"Not anybody from this prison farm."

"Just so," said Howlin.

They continued to watch until the Moon stood completely up off the jumbled horizon.

Tomorrow they were letting him fish for bluegills in one of the prison ponds.

"Thanks, Captain," said Howlin. He handed the guard a stick of Black Jack gum.

"Mind your step," said the guard.

They went back down the hill toward the barracks, their full-moon-lengthened shadows going before them.

When he passed away in his sleep, in the prison-farm hospital, he didn't get much press: he died the same day as Aldous Huxley and John F. Kennedy.

Afterword The Wolf-Man of Alcatraz

It's not hard to come up with snappy, stupid-sounding titles, as here.

What's hard is coming up with a story for it that's not snappy and stupid.

As here.

I tried to imagine what it would be like to live in a world where lycanthropy is real, and you could be incarcerated if you committed a crime while in the ur-state.

(The quote from J. Edgar Hoover is real—real quote was about fellatio, but I changed *that.*) The story flowed from there on May 9–10, 2004.

I did lots of research on Alcatraz (the direct-current electrical system was real: a favorite pastime of prisoners was electroplating their underwear in the toilets, because they were *bored,* and they *could.*)

I re-watched *The Birdman of Alcatraz* to make sure I wasn't kyping anything from there.

When I finished this and read it at an ArmadilloCon, Brad Denton came up afterwards and said, "I saw what you were doing there. Writing a werewolf story where the reader is never sure there's a werewolf or not."

You read it here first.

The Horse of a Different Color (That You Rode in On)

Thanks, Ms. Emshwiller; and Mikes, Walsh and Nelson.

A few years before Manny Marks (that's how he insisted his name be spelled) died at the age of 107, he gave a series of long interviews to Barry Winstead, who was researching a book on the death of vaudeville. Marks was 103 at the time, in the spring of 1990. This unedited tape was probably never transcribed.

Marks: . . . I know it was, because I was playing Conshohocken. Is that thing on? What exactly does it *do?*

Winstead: Are you kidding me?

Marks: Those things have been going downhill since the Dictaphone. How well could that thing record? It's the size of a pack of Luckies . . .

Winstead: Trust me, Mr. Marks.

Marks: Mr. Marx was my father, Samuel "Frenchy" Marx. Call me Manny.

W: Let's start with *that,* then. Why the name change?

M: I didn't want my brothers riding my coattails. They started calling themselves the Four Marx Brothers, after they quit being the Four Nightingales. Milton—Gummo to you—got it out of his system early, after Julius—Groucho to you. Of course, Leo and Arthur had been playing piano in saloons and whorehouses from the time they were ten and eleven. You'll have to tell me whether you think that's show business or not . . .

W: It's making a living with your talent.

M: Barely.

W: You entered show business when?

M: I was fourteen. Turn of the century. I walked out the front door and right onto the stage.

W: Really?

M: There was a three– or four–year period where I made a living with my talent. Like Gene Kelly says, "Dignity, always dignity." Actually, Comden and Green wrote that—it just came out of Kelly's mouth. I was in a couple of acts like the O'Connor/Kelly one at Dead Man's Fang, Arizona, in that movie.

W: With whom?

M: Whom? You sound like Julius.

W: Would I know any of your partners?

M: In what sense?

W: Would I recognize their names?

M: I wouldn't even recognize their names now. That was almost ninety years ago. Give me a break.

W: What was the act?

M: A little of everything. We danced a little, One partner sang a little while I struck poses and pointed. One guy played the *bandoneon*—that's one of those Brazilian accordions with the buttons instead of the keys. I may or may not have acted like a monkey; I'm not saying, and I'm pretty sure there aren't any pictures . . .

W: Gradually you achieved success.

M: Gradually I achieved success.

W: Had your brothers entered show business by then?

M: Maybe. I was too busy playing four-a-days at every tank town in Kansas to notice. A letter caught up with me a couple years on from Mom, talking about Julius stranded in Denver and Milton doing God knows what.

W: Did your mom—Minnie Marx—encourage your career as she later did those of your brothers?

M: I didn't hang around long enough to find out. All I know is I wanted out of my home life.

W: Did Al Shean (of Gallagher and Shean) encourage you?

M: Uncle Al encouraged everybody. "Kid, go out and be bad. Come back and see me when you get good, and I'll help you all I can." Practical man.

W: Your compatriot George Burns said, "Now that vaudeville is dead, there's no place for kids to go and be bad anymore."

M: What about the Fox network?

W: You got him there.

Winstead: So by now you were hoofing as a single.

Marks: No—I moved a little from the waist up, so it wasn't, technically, hoofing. To keep people from watching my feet too much, I told a few jokes. Like Fields in his juggling act or Rogers with his rope tricks. Fields used to do a silent juggling bit. He asked for a raise at the Palace and they said: "You're the highest-paid juggler in the world." He said, "I gotta get a new act."

W: I've heard that story before.

M: Everybody has. I'm just giving you the practicalities of vaudeville. You're the best in the world and you still aren't getting paid enough, you *have* to do something else, too, to get more money. So I was a dancer and—well, sort of a comic. Not a comic dancer—the jokes are in your feet, then. My act: the top part told jokes—the bottom part moved.

Winstead: What was—who do you think was the best? Who summed up vaudeville?

Marks: That's two questions.

W: Okay.

M: Who summed up vaudeville? The answer's the standard one—Jolson, Cantor, Fields, Foy, Brice, Marilyn Miller. They could hold an audience for ten hours if they'd have wanted to. And you can't point to any one thing they had in common. Not one. There are all kinds of being good at what you do . . .

W: And the best?

M: Two acts. You might have run across them, since you write about this stuff for a living. Dybbuk & Wing: a guy from Canarsie and a guy from Shanghai. Novelty dance act. And the Ham Nag. A horse-suit act.

W: I've seen the name on playbills.

M: Ever notice anything about *that?*

W: What?

M: Stick with me and I will astound you later.

W: What, exactly, made them so good?

M: Dybbuk & Wing did, among other things, a spooky act. The theater lights would go down, and they'd be standing there in skeleton costumes—you know, black body suits with bones painted on them. Glowed in the dark. Had a scene drop that glowed in the dark, too. Burying ground—trees, tombstones, and so forth. Like in that later Disney cartoon, what was it?

W: *The Skeleton Dance?*

M: Exactly. Only this was at least twenty years before.

W: So they were like early Melies—the magician filmmaker?

M: No. They were Dybbuk & Wing.

W: I mean, they used the phantasmagorical in the act. What was it like?

M: It wasn't *like* anything. It was terrific, is all I can say. You would swear the bones came apart while they were dancing. I was on bills with them on and off for years. They were the only act I know of that *never* took a bow. The lights didn't come up and they take their skulls off and bow. No matter how much applause. The lights stayed down, the two disappeared, then the lights came back up for the next act. I hated to follow them; so did anyone with a quiet act. They usually put the dog stuff and acrobats on after them, if they had any.

W: *Never* took a bow?

M: Never.

Winstead: What about the horse act?

Marks: The Ham Nag?

W: What did it/they do?

M: It was just the best goddammed horse-suit act there ever was. Or ever could be. I don't know how to begin to describe it, unless you'd say it was like a cartoon horse come to life. Right there, live, on the boards. When you were watching it you felt like you were in another world. Where there were real cartoon horses.

W: Vaudeville was more varied than people of my generation think.

M: It was more varied than even *my* generation could think. You had to see it.

Marks: Dybbuk & Wing set the pattern. Wing—the Chinese guy—never talked. Just like those magicians. Who are they?

Winstead: Penn & Teller?

M: Just like them. I don't mean just in the *act,* like Harpo. I mean, backstage, offstage, in real life. But I don't think he was a mute, either. I played with them for years and never heard him speak.

Like, one time backstage—we'd moved up to three-a-days somewhere—so we had time to kill. It may have been outside the City of Industry or somewhere. There was only one deck of cards in the whole place, and it was our turn to use them between shows.

"Got any Nine of Cups?" I asked.

Wing shook his head no.

"Go Fish," said Dybbuk.

I mean, Wing could have said something if he'd wanted to. It was just *us* in the room . . .

Marks: Okay, the Ham Nag act was, it was always trying to get the one blue apple in a whole pile of green and red ones on a cart. Things kept going wrong. Well, you've seen films from acts back then, like Langdon's exploding car. For some reason, this was hilarious. The Nag made you believe the one goal in its life was to get that apple.

Winstead: You said if I stuck with you, you'd drop a bombshell . . .
Marks: Oh, you *were* paying attention, weren't you?
W: Bombs away.
M: I played with Dybbuk & Wing and the Ham Nag on the Gus Sun circuit out of Chicago for at least four years. I think it was at the Arcadia Theater one afternoon when it suddenly clicked.

You remember I told you to look at those posters in your collection? You'll notice that on every one—don't take my word for it—everywhere the Ham Nag played, Dybbuk & Wing were on the bill . . .

W: You mean . . .
M: It took me four years of being on the same bills with them every day before *I* figured it out. Yeah, they were the Ham Nag, too. It did not come out of their dressing room—they must have changed out in the alleys or the manager's office or somewhere.

That day I went on, did my act, then watched. Dybbuk & Wing were on two spots before me, then suddenly the Ham Nag was on. (The Ham Nag did take four-footed bows and would milk applause. That's why it was called the Ham Nag.) It came offstage. I was going to follow; a chorus girl said something to me; I looked around, and the Ham Nag was gone.

I went to Dybbuk & Wing's dressing room; they were there. Wing was writing a letter and Dybbuk was reading what looked like a two-hundred-year-old book as thick as a cinder block and just as dusty. Like they'd been there all the time.

I finally saw them one night, coming back from the alley after the Ham Nag act. Wing saw me looking at them.

From then on, Dybbuk acted like it was no secret and that I'd known about it all along.

I'm not telling stories out of school here: few people remember either act (though they should), and the acts have been dead half as long as I've been alive. They were supposed to be in that movie I made (*It Goes To Show You,* RKO, 1933, when Manny Marks was forty-seven years old), but they were "hot on the case" by then, as Dybbuk said.

Winstead: What was "the case"?

Marks: Okay. I'm approaching this as an outsider. Ever read *The Waste Land* by T. S. Eliot? Julius and Eliot had a mutual admiration society—they exchanged photos like International Pen Pals.

W: We had to read it in college.

M: Things will be easier if you go home tonight and read it again. Anyway, there's all this grail imagery in it, and other such *trayf.* Only you have to work through it, even if you're a Gentile. So where does that leave *me?* Julius once gave me a book Eliot took a lot of stuff from—somebody named Weston's *From Ritual To Romance.* All this stuff about a wounded king—like Frazer's *The Golden Bough*—look it up.

W: And this has something to do with a horse act?

M: And Dybbuk & Wing's dance act, too. Trust me.

Winstead: So what you're saying here, at the age of 103, is that the Apocalypse may have been averted, and we didn't know it, or *something.*

Marks: Or something. No. I'm saying there was some kind of personal Apocalypse ("That which is revealed when the veil is dropped") involving Dybbuk, Wing, the Ham Nag, a couple other vaudeville types, maybe the Vatican, perhaps Mussolini—Stalin and Hitler for all I know . . .

W: This would have been in . . . ?

M: 1933. When I was making *It Goes To Show You.* Why Dybbuk, Wing, and the Ham Nag couldn't be in the movie.

W: This I'd really like to hear.

M: You will. Hand me that bottle so I can wet my whistle.

Marks: Now you've got me drunk.

Winstead: I don't think so, Mr. Marks. I've seen you drunk.

M: Where?

W: At Walter Woolf King's wake a few years ago.

M: If you were there, you saw me drunk. I was the oldest drunk there. At my age, I'm the oldest drunk *anywhere.*

W: You were going to tell me about the Vatican's and Mussolini's interest in a vaudeville horse-suit act?

M: Was I?

W: I think so. I can't be sure.

M: Okay. Is that thing still on?

W: Yes.

M: Here goes.

Marks: Somewhere around 1927, Coolidge years, the Prohib, vaudeville was already dying. That October would come Jolson in *The Jazz Singer.* It wasn't there yet, but soon the movies would talk, sing, and dance—everything vaudeville could do, only better, because they could spend the money, and every film house could be the Palace, every night.

As I said, you couldn't tell it from *The Jazz Singer*—cantor's son in blackface, jumping around like a fool and disappointing his dad. I saw the play with Jessel back in '25. Trust me, it was *just perfect* for the movies, and more than perfect for Jolson.

But I had seen the end of, as the paper's named, variety. I knew it as soon as Jolson said "You ain't heard nothin' yet!"

So did Dybbuk. So did Wing.

We had to get new acts.

So this is the context I'm talking about.

What Dybbuk & Wing did between their acts was read and write. Wing probably wrote all the letters for them—he did to me, later—I never saw him actually reading, it was Dybbuk who always had a book open. Where he got them, I don't know—maybe they had a secret card, good at any library anywhere. They only seemed to have one or two books with them at a time. Carrying a bunch around in their luggage would have been prohibitive and tiring, especially on the Sun circuit—if you had it good, you only moved every three days; no split-weeks, and only in the relatively bigger towns.

They must have been reading and writing for years before I ever met them. They were on the trail of something. No telling who they corresponded with, or what attention they attracted.

I believe we were playing the Priory Theater in Zion, Illinois, when Pinky Tertulliano joined the bill. He was an albino comic acrobat—like that guy on Broadway now? (1990—ed.)

Winstead: Bill Irwin?

M: That's him. Anyway, since the Flying Cathar Family was already on the bill, they put him between Edfu Yung and Dybbuk & Wing. Edfu Yung was a Sino-Egyptian bird imitator; quite an act. And he threw his call offstage, like Bergen or Señor Wences. You'd swear the stage flies were full of birds. I don't know that Yung and Wing ever talked over their common heritage, since Wing never talked.

Anyway, Tertulliano—who had a very weird act even for vaudeville—and I'm not kidding—was off before Dybbuk & Wing went on, which is the important thing here.

We found out later he'd come straight over from Italy to the Sun circuit in the Midwest, which was unusual unless Gus Sun was your uncle or something—usually you played whatever you could get on the East Coast—unless you were some real big act brought over by an impresario—Wilson Mizener once said an impresario is someone who speaks all languages with a foreign accent—and if that were the case, what's he doing going on between Edfu Yung and Dybbuk & Wing in Zion?

Anyway, things went swimmingly for a week or two, and the whole bill moved to some other town.

I remember things happened on Friday the Thirteenth—it must have been in May, because a couple of weeks later Lindy made his hop—Dybbuk & Wing came off and stuff had been messed with in their dressing room.

Nothing goes through a theater faster than news that there's a sneak thief around. Suddenly keys are needed for the locks on the doors, and people watch each other's places while they're on. Like with the army, where barracks thieves aren't tolerated; if they're found, there's some rough justice dealt out. Signs go up and things get tense.

They never said *what* was messed with or taken; they just filed with the theater, Equity, and Gus Sun himself, and spread the word.

Nobody ever proved anything. Tertulliano left the bill about the time Lindbergh took off for France. Nobody else's stuff was ever taken.

Sometime in June, Wing got a letter with lots of odd stamps and dago-dazzler forms all over it; after he read it he gave it to Dybbuk, who told me: "Never act on a bill with Tertulliano; he's trouble."

That's all he said. Fortunately, I nor anyone else ever had to. Far as I know Pinky left vaudeville and went back to Italy. Which is strange, since he had such a good weird act, like the Flying Cathars all rolled into one.

Marks: . . . so I started noticing stuff about *both* their acts. Like, in the skeleton dance. I told you there were glow-in-the-dark tombstones and things. One was a big sarcophagus, like in those New Orleans cemeteries. On the side of it was the phrase "*Et in Arcadia ego*"—"And I too am in Arcadia" is the usual translation, and people think it means death, too, was in pastoral, idyllic settings. I think it was just an ancient "Kilroy was here," myself.

And the horse-suit act, the Ham Nag. "Why is it always trying to get a blue apple?" I asked. Like something out of Magritte. Who ever heard of a blue apple? (Magritte's favorites were of course green.) Dybbuk didn't say anything; he just handed me what turned out to be the thickest, driest book I had ever tried to read in my life. Honest, I tried.

Wing didn't say anything, of course, he just nodded.

Marks: A week later I brought the book back to them.

"If this is what you guys do for fun," I said, "I think you guys should get out to a movie more often, maybe buy an ice-cream cone.

"You asked," said Dybbuk. "That book explains most of it."

"That book explains my six-day headache," I said. "It's like trying to read Spengler. Better than any Mickey Finn at bedtime. Two paragraphs and I'm sleeping like a baby."

"Sorry," said Dybbuk.

"Besides," I said, "I came from a whole other background. I don't even try to keep *trayf* for the holidays. I'm not a practicing Jew—much less a Christian. People really believe that stuff? The fight between the Catholics and the Freemasons?"

"Some more than others," said Dybbuk. Wing nodded.

"So why put that stuff in the act if it's so important and so secret?"

And Dybbuk said, "If it's *fun,* why do it?"

Marks: I had troubles of my own during all this time, by the way. They tried to slip me down the bill at the next tank town. I needed a new act. The comedy was fine; the dancing and singing never were much, but for vaudeville, it was a wow.

Then I met Marie, who as you know later became Susie Cue.

(Like Burns and Allen, Marks and Susie Cue were a double for the next forty years—in vaudeville, the movie *It Goes To Show You,* in radio and television—anywhere they could work.—ed.)

She was part of a sister act—the *only* good part. I laid eyes on her and that was *it.* I was forty-one years old in '27, she was maybe twenty. In two weeks we were a double, and her sisters were on the way back to Saskatoon.

So my extracurricular interests changed dramatically. So did the finances, thanks to Susie. We became virtually a house-act on the Keith-Albee circuit and did a couple of the last (real) Follies before Ziegfeld croaked, and things got pretty peachy—even with the Crash. Fortunately, as George S. Kaufman said, all my money was tied up in cash, so I came through it okay.

Meanwhile I heard from Julius that my brothers, except for Milton, were making movies, out in Astoria, of their stage plays. I wished them lots of luck.

But that was just another indication variety was dying. I mean, you have a play run for two years on Broadway and you still gotta make movies to make any more money. The movies, now that they talked—for a while there they talked but didn't move much—see *Singin' in the Rain* for that—were raiding everything—plays, novels, short stories, poems, radio—for that matter, radio was raiding right back—in an effort to get what little money people still had left. Movies did it all the time for a dime; vaudeville did it three times a day for fifty cents. Something had to give.

It was me and Susie Cue, and we went into radio.

Meanwhile, Dybbuk & Wing—I supposed it was Wing—were writing to us.

Winstead: So this was . . . ?

Marks: We went into radio in late 1931. So did everybody else.

We'd tried three formats before we found the *right* one.

W: *My Gal Susie Cue?*

M: *My Gal Susie Cue.* The idea was, it was like having lizards live in your vest and I tried to deal with it.

W: Didn't Dybbuk & Wing appear on it?

M: Exactly twice. Tap dance doesn't come across on radio, especially if there's no patter. Even with a live audience all you hear are the taps—a sound-effect man with castanets can do that—and the *oohs* and *ahhs* from the audience.

W: What about the Ham—

M: Even *they* knew a silent horse-suit act wouldn't work on radio. That would have to wait for *Toast of the Town* on TV, but by then they were gone. I don't even know if there's *any* film of the horsey act. I once asked them how they did it so well.

Dybbuk gave the classic answer I've seen attributed to other people. He said: "I'm the front of the horse suit, and I act a whole lot. Wing just acts natural."

Marks: I'm getting ahead of myself. While we were in the Follies and they were still out in the sticks, they wrote me. Letters about other acts, their acts, how bad variety was getting. I did what I could for them, got them a few New York gigs, mostly in olios before movies, that kind of thing. We got together when they were in town. I think they both had crushes on Susie Cue. (Who wouldn't?)

Anyway, when they were on the road they wrote me about their researches, too. It was all too arcane and esoteric for me (those are my two new words of the week from Wordbuilder), but it seemed to keep them happy. They also made noises about "Pinky types" and "priests with tommy-guns" which I took at the time to be hyperbole (my new word from *last* week), but now I'm not so sure.

The trouble with paranoia (as Pynchon and others—yes, I do read the moderns) said, is the deeper you dig, the more you uncover, whether it's there or not. It's the ultimate feedback system—the more you believe, the more you find to believe. I'm not sure, but I think Dybbuk & Wing may have been in the fell clutch of circumstances of their own making.

That was about the gist of the letters—I haven't looked at them since the late '50s—the century's, not mine—in the late 1950s I was seventy—I was drunk one day and dug them out of an old White Owl box I keep them in. Susie Cue came in and found me crying.

"What's the matter, Manfred?"

"Just reliving the glory days," I said.

"*These* are the glory days," she said. Maybe for *her.* She'd just turned fifty.

Anyway, want to jump ahead to where it *really* gets interesting?

W: Sure.

Marks: It was early 1933—the week before FDR was inaugurated and the week *King Kong* premiered (that was something people *really* wanted to see: an ape tearing up Wall Street). We were in LA, making *It Goes To Show You.* Dybbuk & Wing couldn't make it *and* were having their agent return the advance. I've been in show business for ninety years, and there are only two reasons for an act not to show up *and* giving money back: 1) You're dead; 2) Your partner's dead. That's *it.*

I got a confirmation it was them sent the cable.

So no Dybbuk & Wing and no Ham Nag, in their only chance to be filmed. I was more upset about *that* than about the hole in the movie. We had to get two acts for that—that's why The Great Aerius is in there as a comic acrobat and Gandolfo & Castell are in as the dance act. Then we lucked out and got Señor Wences, with Johnny and Pedro in the box. It was his first American movie. You haven't seen weird 'til you've seen Señor Wences in 1933 . . .

Marks: Turn that off a minute.
Winstead: Why?
M: I gotta dig up the letter. I'll read it. It's better than I could tell it.
W: Do you know where it is?
M: Probably it's with the rest. Maybe . . .

Marks: Did you like the lunch?
Winstead: God, I'm stuffed. Did *you* find the letter?
M: I think it was written on 1933 flypaper or something. It's pretty brittle. I think the silverfish have been at it. Yeah, I got it here.
W: Mr. Marks, I want to know exactly how we got off on this.
M: You asked about vaudeville. This is *about* vaudeville.
W: A letter dealing with Christian kook cults is about vaudeville?
M: You'd be surprised. Both contain multitudes.
W: Please read it to me.
M:

Thursday, March 23, 1933

Dear Knowledge-Seeker (they always called me that):
Sorry about missing the movie deal, and (it turns out) we sure could have used the money. I hope you under-

stand. Who did you get to replace us? I hope they turned out boffo.

The easiest way to tell you about it is in order the way it happened. We got to Yakima on the hottest tip we'd ever gotten the week of FDR's inaugural. The tip wasn't about Yakima; it was further west, but this is the closest big-train passenger depot. We'd just done the week in Spokane. Coming in on our heels were the Flying Cathars (you remember them from the Midwest), who are now in a circus (where they came from and where they are now back). John Munster Cathar gave us a letter—an answer to someone we'd written to from Denver.

Let's say it was the most concrete clue we'd ever gotten. Our next booking was in six weeks in Seattle, after we'd supposedly gotten back from doing your movie in Hollywood. We called our agent and had him pick up some one-, two-, and three-nighters between Yakima and Seattle. He cussed us a blue streak for missing the movie *and* having to send the money back. But he got on the horn and got us enough gigs to cover a month of the six weeks anyway.

The first was the next day in a place called Easton, Washington. We went there and did a three-a-day, both acts. Then we got on a spur-line train off the B-N and went to a town called Rosslyn. Which is where we wanted to go in the first place.

An odd thing we noticed as we got there was that there was a priest waiting at the depot. Who he met in fact was another priest, both Catholics. The one he met was young.

Which is strange, since, believe it or not, most of the priests up here are Orthodox—left over from when the Pacific Northwest was Russian, and a lot of Greeks came here around the turn of the century.

Well, we went down to the theater, Rennie's Chateau. We gave the stagehands the drops for the skeleton dance, put our trucks and the horse suit in the dressing room, and asked where we could get breakfast. They told us a block down.

We walked down there. It was cold. Snow was still two feet high off the sidewalks; guys came by talking about how good the salmon run had been last fall. (The only water we could see was a small creek that went off back down toward the Yakima River to the south of us.)

Dybbuk noticed that the two priests were back down the board sidewalk behind us, walking the same way we were, talking with animation and blessing people automatically.

We got to the café, and it was full of lumberjacks, which they call loggers up here. There was a bunch of big tables pushed together in the center of the place, and there were twelve or fifteen of them at it, and they were putting away the grub like it was going out of style. There were plates of biscuits a foot high, and if they had been a family, the guys with the shortest arms would have starved to death.

We sat at the counter on the stools by the pies and cakes and such. Dybbuk got coffee, ham, and scrambled eggs. I got chipped beef on toast, coffee, and a couple of donuts.

The waitress yelled to the cook, "Adam and Eve. Wreck 'em. S.O.S. and a couple sinkers. Two battery acids!"

"Yes, Mabel," yelled one of the cooks, lost in clouds of steam and smells.

"More gravy over here, Mabel!" yelled half the table of lumberjacks.

"Eighty-six the gravy," said the cook, "Unless you wanna wash up. I'm outta big bowls."

"Use that old 'un in the high cabinet," yelled Mabel.

The cook went back and rummaged around. The short-order cook moved to his place at the stove; threw water and flour into the giant skillet the bacon and ham had been cooking in. With his free hand he broke six eggs onto the griddle. The main cook came back, moved exactly into the vacated other cook's place, and stirred the gravy with a big ladle.

He put it into a battered old silver server and passed it through the order-hole to Mabel.

Dybbuk paused with his coffee cup halfway to his lips, rolled his eyes, and focused back on the serving bowl.

Wing (me) followed his gaze. The server was what the ancient Greeks would have called a *krater:* a large, shallow bowl with handles on two sides. There was figurework on the base which extended up the sides of the bowl—it looked like bunches of grapes.

Wing (that's me) nodded to Dybbuk, rolled his eyes, and fixed them on the two priests who had come in and sat down at a window table. They were still talking away and seemed to be paying no attention to anything.

Mabel put the bowl down; six or eight hands filled with biscuits dipped into it and came out with gobs of gravy.

"I s'pose now you'll be wantin' more biscuits?" she asked.

"Mmmmff mmmfnmfs," said the lumberjacks.

"Two doz. hardtack!" she yelled to the cooks.

Back at the dressing room, we thought of a plan. We were going to be at the theater for three days. We got the manager's bill poster to make up a couple of cloth banners advertising the bill. Then we pinned them to both sides of the horse suit. We went out the side door of the theater and up and down the main street, which is called First Street—all the cross-streets are named for states—doing part of the Ham Nag act. We hit the bank, the five-and-dime, the firehouse, the Legion hall; we went past the Masonic Temple across the street from the theater, and of course the café. We went in and bothered Mabel and the cooks. We went back through the kitchen, out the back door, behind the buildings, and back to the theater.

The young priest, who'd been out in front of the theater, gawked at us with the rest of the town (we had quite the little crowd following us down First Street) but stayed in front of the theater, so we figured he wasn't waiting for Dybbuk & Wing.

Later, when we walked back to the hotel on Pennsylvania as ourselves, he followed us as discreetly as a priest can. When we looked outside later, he was still there.

At the theater, Dybbuk went out between our act and the horse act and bought the biggest ceramic bowl the five-and-dime had—it was at least two feet across and weighed a ton. We put it in the cemetery stuff the next performance, leaned it against a tombstone.

The second day the horse suit made more of a nuisance of itself in other parts of town (there were only eight blocks by seven blocks of it, counting Alaska Alley) but ended again annoying the customers and the help at the café.

Once again they were watching the theater—this time the old priest. There was a local-looking kid with him.

When we left for the hotel (as us), it was the kid who wandered that way, and it was either him or some other who stayed outside all night, as far as we knew.

On the third day we took the ceramic bowl with us—me (Wing) carrying it inside his part of the suit. It made for a lumpier horse, I'm sure. After nearly twenty years we move as one, but Dybbuk has to do all the navigating. As they say of huskies, only the lead dog gets a change of scenery.

So we take off down First Street, and even I can tell we're gathering a crowd as we go along. We do some shtick with oil cans at the gas station; I dance around in the back a little, and we move on to the Western Auto hardware store, and then we go down to the café.

This time we came in the back door. "Christ!" says the head cook, "not *again!*" Dybbuk starts farting with stuff (the laughter was at the Ham Nag flipping pancakes with its front hooves) and rummaging through the cabinets (through the slit in the side of the suit I [Wing] saw everybody in the place up against the counter, looking into the kitchen)—the head cook had taken off and thrown down his apron and walked out into the restaurant in disgust, and then—*allez oop!*—the ceramic bowl was outside the Ham Nag and the *krater* was inside, and everybody applauded as we turned and did the double-split bow in the middle of the kitchen floor.

Then we were outside again, at the front door. All I (Wing) heard was Dybbuk say "Trouble!" and grunt before something knocked me off my feet. I jerked back, and some heavy object flattened the suit right between Dybbuk and me. We jumped up and a fist hit me in the jaw and I fell down again. A hand came in the side of the suit and the silver bowl was jerked out of my hands and was gone.

Then something knocked us down again, and we got up and opened the suit to make it a fair fight.

We were surrounded by kids dressed as clowns, including the one I'd seen with the priest. They had what looked like rubber baseball bats and big shoes. There was about half the town around them, clapping and laughing. To them it must have seemed part of the show—the horse suit set on by jokers and clowns. The old priest was standing across from us on the sidewalk, with his hands in his pockets, smiling. He took his hand out and moved it.

I looked way down First Street, and the young priest was just turning out of sight two blocks away with something shiny under his arm.

We got back in the suit and wobbled back toward the theater, the clowns whacking us with rubber bats occasionally. But they hadn't been rubber back in front of the café.

We got back to the dressing room and out of the Ham Nag suit.

"The priest was giving us a Masonic hand signal," Dybbuk said.

Priests don't do that, I (Wing) indicated.

"They do if they're not just priests," Dybbuk said.

We figured, like you did years ago, the kid had doped out we were the Ham Nag too, and the priests laid a plan for us. I'm not sure they knew what we were doing, but someone saw through our misdirection and kept his eye on what was going on.

As Barrymore said, "Never work with kids or dogs."

We almost had it, Knowledge-seeker. Now we'll have to start all over again. After all this time, what's a few years more? I mean, the thing has been around for at least one thousand nine hundred and three years . . .

Here's hoping you and Susie Cue are in the pink of health. We'll be here in Seattle at the Summit on Queen Anne Hill from Thursday 'til the end of next month. Heard your radio show last week; it was a pip.

Yours in knowledge-seeking,

Dybbuk & me (Wing)

—

Winstead: Can you still talk, after reading all that?
Marks: I think so, after I get some of this stuff down. (drinks) There, that's better.
W: I don't know what to say. That was a long session. I don't want to wear you out. Will you feel like talking tomorrow?
M: I think so. You wanna hear about the radio show tomorrow?
W: Whatever you want to talk about. Do you think they ever got it?
M: Got the gravy bowl?
W: The thing they were looking for.
M: Your guess is as good as mine.

*Manny Marks, the last of the Marx Brothers, died three years later at the age of 107. Barry Winstead's book—*I Killed Vaudeville*—was published by Knopf in 1991. Luke H. Dybbuk died in 1942; John P. Wing is still alive, though he retired from performing in the early years of WWII.*

Afterword
The Horse of a Different Color (That You Rode in On)

This is one of the two novelettes I did for CapClave (Baltimore) in 2005.

Michael Walsh proposed "an Ace Double publication—two stories published back to back and upside down—to be given away as part of the membership to the convention."

"If I'm having an Ace Double," I said, "I want a new Emsh cover."

"But . . . ," said Mike, knowing Ed Emshwiller had died a couple of years before.

"Do not concern yourself," I said, like Dan Seymour in *To Have and Have Not.*

I fired off a letter to Carol Emshwiller, all around genius writer and Ed's widow. I'd known they'd met at art school in the 1950s when Carol was floundering around before she realized she was a writer-genius.

"Hey Carol," I asked. "Got any of that art stuff of yours lying around?"

One thing led to another. Eileen Gunn and Pat Murphy, who hike with Carol through Yosemite every summer, made copies of stuff I might use.

I chose four—two backgrounds and two foreground figures—and sent copies to Walsh, who did an admirable job—or would have if his graphic designer's building hadn't gone condo two weeks before the con.

The Double was published about six months after the convention, and copies mailed out to everyone who'd been there.

The house (not mine) I was living in at the time was being renovated by people Not Clear on the Concept, like plugging three fifteen-amp radial saws into the single fifteen-amp outside socket and turning them all on at once, and blowing all the breakers every ten minutes or so.

I wrote this (and its companion) during the carpenter's free-for-all.

I never read *The Da Vinci Code,* but I'd read, years before, the same research Brown had used.

So here it is; a miniature *Da Vinci Code* done shorter and better, and with a pantomime horse, too.

(I'm a big fan of Craig Ferguson's *Late Late Show,* with his horse Secretariat who showed up long after this was written.)

(I'm reminded of Andy Devine's old quote: "I play the front of the horse, and the other guy just acts natural.")

This is probably about the third-densest story I've ever written. In the beginning it was going to be about "The Horse of a Different Color You Heard Tell Of" from *The Wizard of Oz.*

I didn't write *that,* either.

The King of Where-I-Go

Dedicated to Ms. Mary Ethel (Waldrop) Burton Falco Bray Hodnett, my little sister . . .

When I was eight, in 1954, my sister caught polio.

It wasn't my fault, although it took twenty years before I talked myself out of believing it was. See, we had this fight . . .

We were at my paternal grandparents' house in Alabama, where we were always taken in the summer, either being driven from Texas to there on Memorial Day and picked up on the Fourth of July, or taken the Fourth and retrieved Labor Day weekend, just before school started again in Texas.

This was the first of the two times when we spent the whole summer in Alabama. Our parents were taking a break from us for three entire months. We essentially ran wild all that time. This was a whole new experience. Ten years later, when it happened the second time, we would return to find our parents separated—me and my sister living with my mother in a garage apartment that backed up on the railroad tracks, and my father living in what was a former motel that had been turned into day-laborer apartments a half mile away.

Our father worked as an assembler in a radio factory that would go out of business in the early 1960s, when the Japanese started making them better, smaller, and cheaper. Our mother worked in the Ben Franklin 5¢-10¢-25¢ store downtown. Our father had to carpool every day into a Dallas suburb, so he would come and get the car one day a week. We would be going to junior high by then, and it was two blocks away.

But that was in the future. *This* was the summer of 1954.

Every two weeks we would get in our aunt's purple Kaiser and she would drive us the forty-five miles to our maternal grandparents' farm in the next county, and we would spend the next two weeks there. Then they'd come and get us after two weeks and bring us back. Like the movie title says, two weeks in another town.

We were back for the second time at the paternal grandparents' place. It was after the Fourth of July, because there were burned patches on my grandfather's lower field where they'd had to go beat out the fires started by errant Roman candles and skyrockets.

There was a concrete walk up to the porch of our grandparents' house that divided the lawn in two. The house was three miles out of town; sometime in the 1980s the city limits would move past the place when a highway bypass was built to rejoin the highway that went through town and the town made a landgrab.

On the left side of the lawn we'd set up a croquet game (the croquet set would cost a small fortune now, I realize, though neither my grandparents nor aunt was what people called well-off).

My sister and I were playing. My grandfather had gone off to his job somewhere in the county. My grandmother was lying down, with what was probably a migraine, or maybe the start of the cancer that would kill her in a few years. (For those not raised in the South; in older homes the bedroom was also the front parlor—there was a stove, chairs for entertaining, and the beds in the main room of the house.) The bed my grandmother lay on was next to the front window.

My sister, Ethel, did something wrong in the game. Usually I would have been out fishing from before sunup until after dark with a few breaks during the day when I'd have to come back to the house. Breakfast was always made by my grandfather—who had a field holler that carried a mile, which he would let out from the back porch when breakfast was ready, and I'd come reluctantly back from the Big Pond. My grandfather used a third of a pound of coffee a day, and he percolated it for at least fifteen minutes—you could stand a spoon up in it. Then lunch, which in the South is called dinner, when my aunt would come out from her job in town and eat with me and my sister, my grandmother, and any cousins, uncles, or kin who dropped by (always arranged ahead of time, I'm sure), then supper, the evening meal, after my grandfather got home. Usually I went fishing after that, too, until it got too dark to see and the water moccasins came out.

But this morning we were playing croquet and it was still cool so I must have come back from fishing for some reason and been snookered into playing croquet.

"Hey! You can't do that!" I yelled at my sister.

"Do what?" she yelled back.

"Whatever you just did!" I said.

"I didn't do anything!" she yelled.

"You children please be quiet," yelled my grandmother from her bed by the window.

"You cheated!" I yelled at my sister.

"I did not!" she hollered back.

One thing led to another and my sister hit me between the eyes with the green-striped croquet mallet about as hard as a six-year-old can hit. I went down in a heap near a wicket. I sat up, grabbed the blue croquet ball, and threw it as hard as I could into my sister's right kneecap. She went down screaming.

My grandmother was now standing outside the screen door on the porch (which rich people called a verandah) in her housecoat.

"I asked you children to be quiet, please," she said.

"*You* shut up!" said my sister, holding her knee and crying.

My forehead had swelled up to the size of an apple.

My grandmother moved like the wind then, like Roger Bannister, who had just broken the four-minute mile. Suddenly there was a willow switch in her hand and she had my sister's right arm and she was tanning her hide with the switch.

So here was my sister, screaming in two kinds of pain and regretting the invention of language, and my grandmother was saying with every movement of her arm, "Don't-you-ever-tell-me-to-shut-up-young-lady!"

She left her in a screaming pile and went back into the house and lay down to start dying some more.

I was well-pleased, with the casual cruelty of childhood, that I would *never*-ever-in-my-wildest-dreams *ever* tell my grandmother to shut up.

I got up, picked up my rod and tackle box, and went back over the hill to the Big Pond, which is what I would rather have been doing than playing croquet anyway.

That night my sister got what we thought was a cold, in the middle of July.

Next day, she was in the hospital with polio.

My aunt Noni had had a best friend who got poliomyelitis when they were nine, just after WWI, about the time Franklin Delano Roosevelt had gotten his. (Roosevelt had been president longer than anybody, through the Depression the grown-ups were always talking about, and WWII, which was the exciting part of the history books you never *got to* in school. He'd died at the end of the war, more than a year before I was born. Then the president had been Truman, and now it was Ike.) My aunt knew what to do and had Ethel in the hospital quick. It probably saved my sister's life, and at least saved her from an iron lung, if it were going to be *that* kind of polio.

You can't imagine how much those pictures in newsreels scared us all—rows of kids, only their heads sticking out of what looked like long tubular industrial washing machines. Polio attacked many things; it could make it so you couldn't *breathe* on your own—the iron lung was alternately a hypo- and hyperbaric chamber—it did the work of your diaphragm. This still being in vacuum-tube radio times, miniaturization hadn't set in, so the things weighed a ton. They made noises like breathing, too, which made them even creepier.

If you were in one, there was a little mirror over your head (you were lying down) where you could look at yourself; you couldn't look anywhere else.

Normally that summer we would have gone, every three days or so, with our aunt back to town after dinner and gone to the swimming pool in town. But it was closed because of the polio scare, and so was the theater. (They didn't want young people congregating in one place so the disease could quickly spread.) So what you ended up with was a town full of bored schoolkids and teenagers out of school for the summer with *nothing* to do. Not what a Baptist town really cares for.

Of course you could swim in a lake or something. But the nearest lake was miles out of town. If you couldn't hitch a ride or find someone to drive you there, you were S.O.L. You could go to the drive-ins for movies. The nearest one was at the edge of the next county—again you needed someone with wheels, although once there you could sit on top of the car and watch the movie, leaving the car itself to the grownups or older teenage brothers and sisters. (They'd even taken away the seats in front of the snack bar where once you could sit like in a regular theater, only with a cloud of mosquitoes eating you all up, again because of polio.)

Me, I had fishing and I didn't care. Let the town wimps stew in their own juices.

But that was all before my sister made polio up close and personal in the family and brought back memories to my aunt.

But Aunt Noni became a ball of fire.

I couldn't go into the hospital to see my sister, of course—even though I had been right there when she started getting sick. Kids could absolutely not come down to the polio ward. This was just a small county hospital with about forty beds, but it also had a polio ward with two iron lungs ready to go, such was the fear in those days.

My aunt took me to the hospital one day, anyway. She had had a big picture-frame mirror with her, from her house.

"She's propped up on pillows and can't move much," my aunt said. "But I think we can get her to see you."

"Stay out here in the parking lot and watch *that* window," she said. She pointed to one of the half-windows in the basement. I stayed out there until I saw my aunt waving in the window. I waved back.

Then my aunt came out and asked, "Did you see her?"

"I saw you."

"She saw you," she said. "It made her happy." Yeah, I thought, the guy who kneecapped her with the croquet ball.

"I don't know *why,*" I said.

Then Aunt Noni gave me some of my weekly allowance that my parents mailed to her in installments.

I took off to the drugstore like a bullet. I bought a cherry-lime-chocolate Coke at the fountain, and a *Monster of Frankenstein,* a *Plastic Man,* and an *Uncle Scrooge* comic book. That took care of forty of my fifty cents. A whole dime, and nowhere to spend it. If it would have been open, and this had been a Saturday, when we usually got our allowance, I would have used the dime to go to the movies and seen eight cartoons, a Three Stooges short, a newsreel, a chapter of a serial, some previews, and a double feature: some SF flick and a Guy Madison movie if I was lucky, a couple of Westerns if I wasn't.

But it was a weekday, and I went back to the office where my aunt Noni was the Jill-of-all-trades plus secretary for a one-man business for forty-seven years (it turned out). It was upstairs next to the bank. Her boss, Mr. Jacks, lived in the biggest new house in town (until, much later, the new doctor in town built a house out on the highway modeled on Elvis' Graceland). Mr. Jacks' house, as fate would have it, was situated on a lot touching my aunt's, only set one house over and facing the other street back.

He wasn't in; he usually wasn't in the office when I was there. Aunt Noni was typing like a bunny, a real blur from the wrists down. She was the only one in the family who'd been to college. (Much later I would futz around in one for five years without graduating.) She could read, write, and speak Latin, like I later could. She read books. She had the librarian at the Carnegie Library in town send off to Montgomery for books on polio; they'd arrived while I was having the Coca-Cola comic-book orgy, and she'd gone to get them when the librarian had called her. There was a pile on the third chair in the office.

I was sitting in the second one.

"I want to know," she said as she typed without looking at her shorthand pad or the typewriter, "enough so that I'll know if someone is steering me wrong on something. I don't want to know enough to become pedantic—"

"Huh?" I asked.

She nodded toward the big dictionary on the stand by the door.

I dutifully got up and went to it.

"P-?"

"P-E-D-A," said my aunt, still typing.

I looked it up. "Hmmm," I said. "Okay." Then I sat back down.

"They're talking like she won't walk again without braces or crutches. That's what they told my friend Frances in nineteen and twenty-one," she said. "You see her motorboatin' all around town now. She only limps a little when she gets really tired and worn out."

Frances worked down at the dress shop. She looked fine except her right leg was a little thinner than her left.

"My aim is to have your sister walking again by herself by next summer."

"Will it happen?"

"If I have anything to do with it, it will," said Aunt Noni.

I never felt so glum about the future as I did sitting there in my aunt's sunny office that July afternoon. What if she were wrong? What if my sister, Ethel, never walked again? What would her life be like? Who the hell would I play croquet with, in Alabama in the summer, if not her, when I wasn't fishing?

Of course, a year later, the Salk vaccine was developed and tried out and started the end of polio. And a couple of years after that came the Sabin oral vaccine, which they gave to you on sugar cubes and which tasted like your grandfather's old hunting socks smelled, which really ended the disease.

We didn't know any of that then. And the future didn't help my sister *any* right then.

My parents had of course taken off work and driven from Texas at the end of the first week; there were many family conferences to which the *me* part of the family was not privy. My parents went to see her and stayed at the hospital.

What was decided was that my sister was to remain in Alabama with my grandparents for the next year and that I was to return to my dead hometown in Texas with my parents and somegoddamnhow survive the rest of the summer there.

My sister, Ethel, would be enrolled in school in Alabama, provided she was strong enough to do the schoolwork. So I fished the Big Pond and the Little Pond one last time, 'til it was too dark to see and the bass lost interest in anything in the tackle box, and I went over the low hill to my grandparents' house, robbed of a summer.

Next morning we got the car packed, ready to return to Texas, a fourteen-hour drive in a flathead 6 1952 Ford. Then we stopped by the hospital. Aunt Noni was already there, her purple Kaiser parked by the front door. My parents went in; after a while Aunt Noni waved at the window, then I saw a blur in the mirror and a shape and I waved and waved and jumped up and down with an enthusiasm I did not feel. Then I got in the car and we went back to Texas.

Somehow, I did live through that summer.

One of the things that got me through it was the letters my aunt took down from my sister and typed up. The first couple were about the hospital, 'til they let her go, and then about what she could see from the back room of my grandparents' house.

We'd usually only gone to Alabama for the summer, and sometimes rushed trips at Christmas, where we were in the car fourteen hours (those days the Interstate Highway System was just a gleam in Ike's eye—so he could fight a two-front war and not be caught short moving stuff from one coast to the other like they had in the Korean War when he was running Columbia University in NYC). We stayed at our grandparents' places Christmas Eve and on Christmas morning and then drove fourteen hours back home just in time for my parents to go to work the day after Christmas.

So I'd never seen Alabama in the fall or the spring. My sister described the slow change from summer to fall there after school started (in Texas it was summer 'til early October, and you had the leaves finish falling off the trees the third week of December and new buds coming out the second week of January). She wrote of the geese she heard going over on the Mississippi flyway.

She complained about the schoolwork; in letters back to her I complained about *school itself:* the same dorks were the same dorks, the same jerks the same jerks, the same bullies still bullies. And that was third grade. Then, you always think it's going to change the next year, until you realize: these jerks are going to be the same ones I'm stuck with the rest of their lives. (As "Scoop" Jackson the senator would later say—it's hard to turn fifty-five and realize the world is being run by people you used to beat up in the fourth grade.)

Third grade was the biggest grind of my life. My sister was finding Alabama second grade tough, too; there was no Alamo, no Texas-under-six-flags. In Alabama there was stealing land from the Choctaws and Cherokees, there was the cotton gin and slavery, there was the War for Southern Independence, and then there was the boll weevil. That was about it. No Deaf Smith, no Ben Milam, no line drawn in the dirt with the sword, no last battle of the Civil War fought by two detachments who didn't *know* the war was over, six weeks after Appomattox; no Spindletop, no oil boom, no great comic-book textbook called *Texas History Movies* which told you everything in a casually racist way but which you remembered better than any textbook the rest of your life.

I told her what I was doing (reading comics, watching TV) and what I caught in the city park pond or the creek coming out of it. It was the fifties in Texas. There was a drought; the town well had gone dry, and they were digging a lake west of town which, at the current seven inches of rain a year, would take twenty-two years to fill up, by which time we'd all be dead.

I told her about the movies I'd seen once the town's lone theater had opened back up. (There were three drive-ins: one in the next town west, with a great neon cowboy round-up scene on the back of the screen, facing the highway—one guy strummed a green neon guitar, a red neon fire burned at the chuck wagon, a vacquero twirled a pink neon lasso; one at the west edge of our town; and one near the next town to the east.)

Anyway, I got and wrote at least one letter a week to and from my sister; my aunt wrote separate letters to me and my parents; they called each other at least once a week.

Somehow, Christmas dragged its ass toward the school year; my parents decided we'd go to Alabama during the break and see my sister and try to have a happy holiday.

My sister was thinner and her eyes were shinier. She looked pretty much the same except her left leg was skinny. She was propped up in bed. Everybody made a big fuss over her all the time. There was a pile of Christmas presents for her out under the tree in the screened-in hall that would choke a mastodon.

I was finally in her room with no one else there.

"Bored, huh?" I asked.

"There's too many people playing the damned fool around here for me to get bored," she said.

"I mean, outside of Christmas?"

"Well, yeah. The physical therapist lady comes twice a day usually and we go through *that* rigmarole."

"I hope people got you lots of books," I said.

"I've read so many books I can't see straight, Bubba."

"Have you read *All About Dinosaurs?*" I asked.

"No."

"I've got my copy with me. You can read it but I gotta have it back before we leave. I stood in a Sears and Roebuck store in Ft. Worth for six hours once while they shipped one over from the Dallas warehouse. The last truck came in and the book wasn't there. They were out and didn't know it. I'd saved up my allowance for *four weeks!* Without movies or comic books! I told anybody who would *listen* about it. A week later one came in the mail. Aunt Noni heard the story and ordered it for me."

"Bless her heart."

"I'm real sorry all this happened, Sis," I said, before I knew I was saying it. "I wish we hadn't fought the day before you got sick."

"What? What fight?"

"The croquet game. You hit me."

"You hit me!" she said.

"No. You backsassed Mamaw. *She* hit you."

"Yes, she did," said my sister, Ethel.

"Anyway, I'm sorry."

"It wasn't your fault," she said.

I really was going to talk to her more but some damnfool uncle came in wearing his hat upside down to make her laugh.

My sister grew up and. walked again, and except for a slight limp and a sometime windmilling foot (like my aunt's friend Frances when she was *very* tired), she got around pretty well, even though she lost most of a year of her life in that bed in Alabama.

I remember walking with her the first day of school when she had come back to Texas and was starting third grade.

"Doing okay?" I asked. We lived three whole blocks from school then, but I wanted her to take it slow and not get too tired.

"Yeah. Sure," she said.

I remember the day they handed out the permission forms for the Salk polio vaccine, which was a big shot with a square needle in the meat of your arm.

My sister laughed and laughed. "Oh, bitter irony!" she said "Oh, ashes and dust!"

"Yeah," I said, "well . . ."

"Have Mom and Pop sign yours *twice,*" she said. "At least it'll do *you* some good."

"Once again, Sis, I'm sorry."

"Tell *that* to the school nurse," she said.

At some point, when we were in our late teens, we were having one of those long philosophical discussions brothers and sisters have when neither has a date and you're too damned tired from the school week to get up off your butt and go out and do something on your own, and the public library closed early. Besides, your folks are yelling at each other in their bedroom.

The Time Machine was one of my favorite movies (they all are). I had the movie tie-in paperback with the photo of Rod Taylor on the back; the *Dell Movie Classic* comic book with art by Alex Toth, and the *Classics Illustrated* edition with art by Lou Cameron—it had been my favorite for years before the movie had come out in 1960.

"What would I do," I repeated Ethel's question, "if I could travel in time? Like go see dinosaurs, or go visit the spaceport they're going to build just outside this popsicle burg?

"Most people would do just what I'd do: first I'd go to the coin shop, buy ten early 1930s Mercury dimes, then go back to 1938 and buy ten copies of *Action Comics* #1 with Superman's first story, and then I'd go write mash notes to Eve Arden."

I'd just finished watching reruns of *Our Miss Brooks* on TV.

"No," she said. "I mean, really?"

"No," I said. "I mean, *really*."

"Wouldn't you try to stop Oswald?" she asked. "Go strangle Hitler in his cradle?"

"You didn't ask 'What would you do if you could travel in time to make the world a better place?' You asked 'What would you do if you could travel in time?'"

"Be that way," she said.

"I *am* that way."

And then she went off to work at some Rhine-like lab in North Carolina. That's not what she set out to do—what she set out to do was be a carhop, get out of the house and our live local version of the *Bickersons*. (Bickering=Pow! Sock! Crash!)

She first worked as a carhop in town, from the time she was fourteen, and then she got the real glamour job over in Dallas at the biggest drive-in cafe there, twenty-five carhops, half of them on skates (not *her*). She moved in with two other carhops there. A few months later, King and Bobby Kennedy got killed and half the U.S. burned down.

Something happened at the cafe—I never found out *exactly* what. But a week later she called home and said this research lab was flying her to North Carolina for a few days (she'd never flown before). And then she left.

I started getting letters from her. By then our parents had gotten a divorce; I was living in the house with my father (who would die in a few months of heart failure—and a broken heart). My mom had run off with the guy she'd been sneaking around with the last couple of years, and we weren't talking much. I was in college and seeing the girl I would eventually marry, have a kid with, and divorce.

My sister told me *they* were really interested in her; that other institutes were trying to get her to come over to them and that she wasn't the only polio survivor there. My first thought was—what's going on? Is this like Himmler's interest in twins and gypsies, or was this just statistically average? This was the late '60s; lots of people our age had polio before 1955, so maybe that was it?

Her letters were a nice break in the college routine—classes, theater, part-time thirty-six-hour-a-week job. Of course I got an ulcer before I turned twenty-two. (Later it didn't keep me from being drafted; it had gotten better after I quit working thirty hours a week in theater plus the job plus only sleeping between three and six a.m. seven days a week.)

"The people here are nice," she said. "The tests are fun, except for the concentration. I get headaches like Mamaw used to get, every other day." She sent me a set of the cards—Rhine cards. Circle, triangle, star, square, plus sign, wavy horizontal lines. They had her across the table from a guy who turned the cards, fifty of them, randomly shuffled. She was supposed to intuit (or receive telepathically) which cards he'd turned over. She marked the symbol she thought it was. There was a big high partition across the middle of the table—she could barely see the top of the guy's head. Sometimes she was the one turning the cards and tried to send messages to him. There were other, more esoteric ones—the tests were supposed to be scientific *and* repeatable.

From one of her letters:

> I don't mind the work here, and if they prove something by it, more's the better. What I *do* mind is that all the magazines I read here think that if there is something to extrasensory perception, then there also has to be mental contact with UFOs (*what* UFOs?) and the Atlanteans (*what* Atlantis?) and mental death rays and contact with the spirit world (*what* spirit world?).
>
> I don't understand that; proving extrasensory perception only proves *that* exists, and they haven't even proved *that* yet. Next week they're moving me over to the PK unit—PsychoKinesis. Moving stuff at a distance without, as Morbius said, "instrumentality." That's more like what happened at the drive-in anyway. They wanted to test me for this stuff first. Evidently I'm not very good at this. Or I'm the same as everybody else, except the ones they catch cheating, by what they call reading the other person—physical stuff like in poker, where somebody always lifts an eyebrow when the star comes up—stuff like that.

Will write to you when I get a handle on this PK stuff.

Your sis,
Ethel

"You would have thought I set off an atom bomb here," her next letter began. She then described what happened and the shady-looking new people who showed up to watch her tests.

Later, they showed her some film smuggled out of the USSR of ladies shaped like potatoes doing hand-*schtick* and making candles move toward them.

My sister told them her brother could do the same thing with 2-lb test nylon fishing line.

"If I want *that* candle *there* to move over here, I'll do it without using my hands," she'd said.

And then, the candle *didn't* move.

"They told me then my abilities may lie in some other area; that the cafe incident was an anomaly, or perhaps someone else, a cook or another carhop had the ability; it had just happened to her because she was the one with the trays and dishes.

"Perhaps," she had told them, "you were wrong about me entirely and are wasting your motel and cafeteria money and should send me back to Texas Real Soon. Or maybe I have the ability to move something *besides* candles, something no one else ever had. Or maybe we are just all pulling our puds." Or words to that effect.

A couple of days later she called me on the phone. The operator told her to deposit $1.15. I heard the *ching* and chime of coins in the pay phone.

"Franklin," said Ethel.

She *never* called me by my right name; I was Bubba to everyone in the family.

"Yes, Sis, what is it?"

"I think we had a little breakthrough here. We won't know til tomorrow. I want you to know I love you."

"What the hell you talkin' about?"

"I'll let you know," she said.

Then she hung up.

The next day was my usual Wednesday, which meant I wouldn't get any sleep. I'd gotten to bed the night before at 2 a.m. I was in class by 7 a.m. and had three classes and lab scattered across the day. At 6 p.m. I drove to the regional newspaper plant that printed all the suburban dailies. I was a linotype operator at minimum wage. The real newspaper that owned all the suburban ones was a union shop, and the guys there made $3.25 an hour in 1968 dollars. I worked a twelve-hour shift (or a little less if we got all the type set early) three nights a week, Mon.-Wed.-Fri. That way, not only did you work for $1.25 an hour, they didn't owe you for overtime unless you pulled more than a sixteen-hour shift one night—and nobody ever did.

Linotypes were mechanical marvels—so much so that Mergenthaler, who finally perfected it, went slap-dab crazy before he died. It's like being in a room of mechanical monsters who spit out hot pieces of lead (and sometimes hot lead itself all over you—before they do that, they make a distinctive noise and you've got a second and a half to get ten feet away; it's called a backspill).

Once all linotype was set by hand, by the operators. By the time I came along, they had typists set copy on a tape machine. What came out there was perforated tape, brought into the linotype room in big, curling strands. The operator—me—put the front end of the tape into a reader-box built onto the keyboard, and the linotype clicked away like magic. The keys depressed, lines of type-mold keys fell into place from a big magazine above the keyboard; they were lifted up and moved over to the molder against the pot of hot lead; the line was cast, an arm came down, lifted the letter matrices up, another rod pushed them over onto an endless spiraled rod, and they fell back into the typecase when the side of the matrix equaled the space on the typecase, and the process started all over. If the tape code was wrong and a line went too long, you got either type matrices flying everywhere as the line was lifted to the molder, or it went over and you got a backspill and hot lead flew across the room.

Then you had to turn off the reader, take off the galley where the slugs of hot type came off to cool, open up the front of the machine, clean all the lead off with a wire brush, put it back together, and start the tape reader back up. When the whole galley was set and cool, you pulled a proof on a small rotary press and sent it back to the typists, where corrections would come back on shorter and shorter pieces of paper tape. You kept setting and inserting the corrections and throwing away the bad slugs until the galley was okayed; then you pulled a copy of the galley and sent it up to the composing room where they laid out the page of corrected galley, shot a page on a plate camera, and made a steel plate from that; that was put on the web press and the paper was run off and sent out to newsboys all over three counties.

It was a noisy, nasty twelve-hour hell with the possibility of being hit in the face with molten lead or asphyxiating when, in your copious free time, you took old dead galleys and incorrect slugs back to the lead smelter to melt down and then ladled out molten lead into pig-iron molds which, when cooled down, you took and hung by the hole in one end to the chain above the pot on each linotype—besides doing everything else it did, the machine lowered the lead pigs into the pots by a ratchet gear each time it set a line. No wonder Mergenthaler went mad.

I did all that twelve hours a night three nights a week for five years, besides college. There were five linotypes in the place, including one that Mergenthaler himself must have made around 1880, and usually three of them were down at a time with backspills or other problems.

Besides that, there were the practical jokers. Your first day on the job you were always sent for the type-stretcher, all over the printing plant. "Hell, I don't know *who* had that last!" they'd say. "Check the composing room." Then some night the phone would ring in the linotype room; you'd go to answer it and get an earful of printers' ink, about the consistency of axle grease. Someone had slathered a big gob on the earpiece and called you from somewhere else in the plant. *Nyuk nyuk nyuk.*

If you'd really pissed someone off (it never happened to me), they'd wait for a hot day and go out and fill all four of your hubcaps with fresh shrimp. It would take two or three days before they'd really stink; you'd check everywhere in the car but the hubcaps; finally something brown would start running from them and you'd figure it out. *Nyuk nyuk nyuk.*

That night I started to feel jumpy. Usually I was philosophical: *Why, this is hell, nor am I out of it.* Nothing was going on but the usual hot, repetitious drudgery. Something felt wrong. My head didn't exactly hurt, but I knew it was *there.* Things took on a distancing effect—I would recognize that from dope, later on. But there was no goofer dust in my life then. Then I noticed everybody else was moving and talking faster than normal. I looked at the clock with the big sweep second-hand outside the linotype room. It had slowed to a crawl.

I grabbed on to the bed of the cold iron proof-press and held on to it. Later, when I turned fifty or so, I was in a couple of earthquakes on the West Coast, but they were nothing compared to what I was feeling at that moment.

One of the tape compositor ladies, a blur, stopped in front of me and chirped out "Doyoufeelallright, Frank?"

"Justa headacheI'llbeokay," I twittered back.

I looked at the clock again.

The sweep-hand stopped. I looked back into the linotype room.

People moved around like John Paul Stapp on the *Sonic Wind* rocket sled.

I looked at the clock again. The second hand moved backward.

And then the world blurred all out of focus and part of me left the clanging clattering linotypes behind.

I looked around the part of town I could see. (What was I doing *downtown?* Wasn't I at *work?*) The place looked like it did around 1962. The carpet shop was still in business—it had failed a few months before JFK was shot. Hamburgers were still four for a dollar on the menus outside the cafes. The theater was showing *Horror Chamber of Dr. Faustus* and *The Manster,* which was a 1962 double feature. Hosey the usher was leaving in his '58 Chevy; he quit working at the theater in 1964, I knew. I had a feeling that if I walked one block north and four blocks west I could look in the window of a house and see myself reading a book or doing homework. I sure didn't want to do *that.*

Then the plant manager was in front of me. "Hey! You've got a backspill on #5, that crappy old bastard, and #3's quit reading tape."

"Sorry," I said. "I just got a splitting headache for a minute. Got any aspirin?" I asked, taking the galley off #5.

"Go ask one of the women who's having her period," he said. "I just took all the aspirin in the place. The publisher's *all over* my ass this week. Why, I don't know. I robbed the first-aid kit: don't go there."

"That would have been my next stop," I said. I brushed a cooled line of lead off the keyboard and from the seat and up the back of the caster chair in front of the linotype. I closed the machine back up and started it up and went over and pounded on the reader box of #3. It chattered away.

For a while I was too busy to think about what had happened.

"Feeling a little weird?" asked my sister, this time on a regular phone.

"What the hell happened?"

"Talk to this man," she said.

She put on some professor whose name I didn't catch.

He asked me some questions. I told him the answers. He said he was sending a questionnaire. My sister came back on.

"*I* think *they* think I gave you a bad dream two thousand miles away," she said. "That would be a big-cheese deal to them."

"What do *you* think?" I asked. "I saw Hosey."

"Either way, you would have done *that*," she said.

"What do you mean, *either way?* Why are you involving *me?* Is this *fun?*"

"Because," she said, "you're my brother and I love you."

"Yeah, well . . . ," I said. "Why don't you mess with someone you *don't* like? Who's that guy who left you in Grand Prairie to walk home at 5 a.m.?"

"I killed him with a mental lightning bolt yesterday," she said. Then, "Just kidding.

"Well, I'm glad you're just kidding, because I just *shit my pants.* I don't want to ever feel like I did last night, again, ever. It was creepy."

"Of course it was creepy," she said. "We're working at the frontiers of science here."

"Are you on the frontiers of science there," I asked, "or . . ."

She finished the sentence with me: ". . . are we just pulling our puds?" She laughed. "I don't have a clue. They're trying to figure out how to do this scientifically. They may have to fly you in."

"No, thanks!" I said. "I've got a life to live. I'm actually dating a real-live girl. I'm also working myself to death. I don't have time for hot dates with Ouija boards, or whatever you're doing there. Include me out."

She laughed again. "We'll see."

"No you won't! Don't do this to me. I'm—"

There was a dial tone.

So the second time I knew what was happening. I was at home. I felt the distancing effect; the speeding up of everything around, except the kitchen clock. It was the kind where parts of numbers flipped down, an analog readout. It slowed to a crawl. The thin metal strips the numbers were painted on took a real long time before they flipped down.

A bird rocketed through the yard. The neighbor's dog was a beige blur. I could barely move. My stomach churned like when I was on the Mad Octopus at the Texas State Fair. The clock hung between 10:29 and 10:50 a.m. Then it was 10:29. 10:28. 10:27. Then the readout turned into a high whining flutter.

This time everything was bigger. Don't ask *me* why. I was at my favorite drugstore, the one next to the theater. The drugstore was at the corner of Division and Center Street. I glanced at a newspaper. June 17, 1956. If memory serves, I would have been over in Alabama at the time, so I wouldn't be running into myself. I reached in my pocket and looked at my change. Half of it hadn't been minted yet. (How was *that* possible?) The guy at the register ignored me—he'd seen me a million times, and I wasn't one of the kids he had to give the Hairy Eyeball to. When I came in, I came to buy.

I looked at the funny book rack. Everything except the Dell Comics had the Comics Code Seal on them, which meant they'd go to Nice Heaven. No zombies, no monsters, no blood, no*Blackhawks* fighting the Commies, who used stuff that melts tanks, people—everything but wood. No vampires "saaaaking your blaaad." Dullsville. I picked up a *Mad* magazine, which was no longer a comic book, so it wouldn't be under the Comics Code, but had turned into a 25¢—*What, me cheap?*—magazine. It had a Kelly Freas cover of Alfred E. Neuman.

I fished out a 1952 quarter and put it down by the register. There wasn't any sales tax in Texas yet. Fifty years later, we would be paying more than New York City.

I looked at the theater marquee when I stepped outside. *Bottom of the Bottle* and *Bandido*—one with Joseph Cotten and Richard Egan, the other with Glenn Ford and Gilbert Roland. I'd seen them later, bored by the first except for a storm scene, and liked the second because there were lots of explosions and Browning .50 caliber machine guns. Nothing for me there.

I walked down toward Main Street.

There was a swooping sensation and a flutter of light and I was back home.

The analog readout on the clock clicked to 10:50 a.m.

I went to the coin shop. I went to my doctor's office. I went to a couple of other places. I actually had to lie a couple of times, and I used one friendship badly, only *they* didn't know, but I did.

Then I found the second letter my sister had sent me from North Carolina and got the phone number of the lab. I called it the next morning. It took a while, but they finally got Ethel to the phone.

"Feeling okay?" she asked.

"Hell no," I said. "I'm not having *any* fun. At least let me have *fun.* Two days from now give me an hallucination about Alabama. In the summer. I want to at least see if the fishing is as good as I remember it."

"So it is written," she said, imitating Yul Brynner in *The Ten Commandments,* "so it shall be done."

I knew it really didn't matter, but I kept my old fiberglass spinning rod, with its Johnson Century spinning reel, and my old *My Buddy* tackle box as near me as I could the next two days. Inside the tackle box with all the other crap were three new double-hook rigged rubber eels, cheap as piss in 1969, but they cost $1.00 each in 1950s money when they'd first come out.

This time I was almost ready for it and didn't panic when the thing came on. I rode it out like the log-flume ride out at Six Flags Over Texas, and when the clock outside the college classroom started jumping backward, I didn't even get woozy. I closed my eyes and made the jump myself.

I was at the Big Pond and had made a cast. A two-pound bass had taken the rubber eel. The Big Pond was even bigger than I remembered (although I knew it was only four acres). I got the bass in and put it on a stringer with its eleven big clamps and swivels between each clamp on the chain. I put the bass out about two feet in the water and put the clamp on the end of the stringer around a willow root.

Then I cast again, and the biggest bass I had ever had took it. There was a swirl in the water the size of a #5 washtub, and I set the hook.

I had him on for maybe thirty seconds. He jumped in the shallow water as I reeled. He must have weighed ten pounds. When he came down there was a splash like a cow had fallen into the pond.

Then the rubber eel came sailing lazily out of the middle of the commotion, and the line went slack in a backflowing arc. It (probably *she*) had thrown the hook.

There was a big V-wake heading for deeper water when the bass realized it was free.

I was pissed off at myself. I picked up the stringer with the two-pound bass (which now didn't look as large as it had five minutes ago) and my tackle box and started off over the hill back toward my grandparents' house.

I walked through the back gate, with its plowshare counterweight on the chain that kept it closed. I took the fish off the stringer and eased it into the seventy-five gallon rainbarrel, where it started to swim along with a catfish my uncle had caught at the Little Pond yesterday. In the summer, there was usually a fish fry every Friday. We got serious about fishing on Thursdays. By Friday there would be fifteen or twenty fish in the barrel, from small bluegills to a few crappie to a bunch of bass and catfish. On Fridays my uncle would get off early, start cleaning fish, heating up a cast-iron pot full of lard over a charcoal fire and making up batter for the fish and hush puppies. Then, after my grandfather came in, ten or eleven of us would eat until we fell over.

Later the cooled fish grease would be used to make dogbread for my grandfather's hounds. You didn't waste much in Alabama in those days.

I washed my hands off at the outside faucet and went through the long hall from the back door, being quiet, as the only sound in the house was of SuZan, the black lady who cooked for my grandmother, starting to make lunch. I looked into the front room and saw my grandmother sleeping on the main bed.

I went out onto the verandah. I'd taken stuff out of the tackle box in the back hall, when I'd leaned my fishing rod up against a bureau, where I kept it ready to go all summer.

I was eating from a box of Domino sugar cubes when I came out. My sister was in one of the Adirondack-type wooden chairs, reading a *Katy Keene* comic book; the kind where the girl readers sent in drawings of dresses and sunsuits they'd designed for Katy. The artist redrew them when they chose yours for a story, and they ran *your* name and address printed beside it so other Katy Keene fans could write you. (Few people know it, but that's how the internet started.)

She must have been five or six—before she got sick. She was like a sparkle of light in a dark world.

"Back already?" she asked. "Quitter."

"I lost the biggest fish of my life," I said. "I tried to horse it in. I should have let it horse me but kept control, as the great A. J. McClane says in *Field and Stream,*" I said. "I am truly disappointed in my fishing abilities for the first time in a long time."

"Papaw'll whip your ass if he finds out you lost that big fish he's been trying to catch," she said. "He would have gone in after it, if he ever had it on." He *would have,* too.

"Yeah, he's a cane-pole fisherman, the best there ever was, but it was too shallow there for him to get his minnow in there with a pole. It was by that old stump in the shallow end." Then I held up the sugar-cube box.

"Look what I found," I said.

"Where'd you get those?"

"In the old chiffarobe."

"SuZan'll beat your butt if she finds you filchin' sugar from her kitchen."

"Probably some of Aunt Noni's for her tea. She probably bought it during the Coolidge Administration and forgot about it." Aunt Noni was the only person I knew in Alabama who drank only one cup of coffee in the morning, and then drank only tea, iced or hot, the rest of the day.

"Gimme some," said Ethel.

"What's the magic word?"

"Please *and* thank you."

I moved the box so she took the ones I wanted her to. She made a face. "God, that stuff is old," she said.

"I *told* you they was," I said.

"Gimme more. Please," she said. "Those are better." Then: "I've read this *Katy Keene* about to death. Wanna play croquet 'til you get up your nerve to go back and try to catch that fish before Papaw gets home?"

"Sure," I said. "But that fish will have a sore jaw 'til tomorrow. He'll be real careful what he bites the rest of the day. I won't be able to tempt him again until tomorrow."

We started playing croquet. I had quite the little run there, making it to the middle wicket from the first tap. Then my sister came out of the starting double wicket, and I could tell she was intent on hitting my ball, then getting to send me off down the hill. We had a rule that if you were knocked out of bounds, you could put the ball back in a mallet-head length from where it went out.

But if you hit it hard enough, the ball went out of bounds, over the gravel parking area, down the long driveway, all the way down the hill and out onto Alabama Highway 12. You had to haul your ass all the way down the dirt drive, dodge the traffic, retrieve the ball from your cousin's front yard, and climb all the way back up to the croquet grounds to put your ball back into play.

My sister tapped my ball at the end of a long shot. She placed her ball against it, and put her foot on top of her croquet ball. She lined up her shot. She took a practice tap to make sure she had the right murderous swing.

"Hey!" I said ."My ball moved! That counts as your shot!"

"Does not!" she yelled.

"Yes it does!" I yelled.

"Take your next shot! *That* counted!" I added.

"It did not!" she screamed.

"You children be quiet!" my grandmother yelled from her bed of pain.

About that time was when Ethel hit me between the eyes with the green-striped croquet mallet; I kneecapped her with the blue croquet ball, and, with a smile on my swelling face as I heard the screen door open and close, I went away from there.

This time I felt like I had been beaten with more than a mallet wielded by a six-year-old. I felt like I'd been stoned by a crowd and left for dead. I was dehydrated. My right foot hurt like a bastard, and mucus was dripping from my nose. I'm pretty sure the crowds in the hall as classes let out noticed—they gave me a wide berth, like I was a big ugly rock in the path of migrating salmon.

I got home as quickly as I could, cutting *History of the Totalitarian State 405,* which was usually one of my favorites.

I called the lab long distance. Nobody knew about my sister. Maybe it was her day off. I called the Motel 6. Nobody was registered by her name." The manager said, "Thank you for calling Motel 6." Then he hung up.

Maybe she'd come back to Dallas. I called her number there.

"Hello," said somebody nice.

"Is Ethel there?"

"Ethel?"

"Yeah, Ethel."

"Oh. That must have been Joanie's *old* roommate."

I'd met Joanie once. "Put Joanie on, please?" I asked.

She was in, and took the phone.

"Joanie? Hi. This is Franklin—Bubba—Ethel's brother."

"Yeah?"

"I can't get ahold of her in North Carolina."

"Why would you be calling her *there*, honey?"

"'Cause that's where she was the last two weeks."

"I don't know about *that*. But she moved out of *here* four months ago. I got a number for her, but she's never there. The phone just rings and rings. If you happen to catch her, tell her she still owes me four dollars and thirty-one cents on that last electric bill. I'm workin' mostly days now, and I ain't waitin' around two hours to see her. She can leave it with Steve; he'll see I get it."

"Steve. Work. Four dollars," I mumbled.

She gave me the number. The prefix meant south Oak Cliff, a suburb that had been eaten by Dallas.

I dialed it.

"Ethel?"

"Who is this? What the hell you want? I just worked a double shift."

"It's Bubba," I said.

"Brother? I haven't heard from you in a month of Sundays."

"No wonder. You're in North Carolina; you come back *without* telling me; you didn't tell me you'd moved out from Joanie's . . ."

"What the hell you mean, North Carolina?! I been pullin' double shifts for three solid weeks—I ain't had a day off since September 26th. I ain't never been to North Carolina in my life."

"Okay. First, Joanie says you owe her $4.31 on the electric bill . . ."

"Four thirty-one," she said, like she was writing it down. "I'll be so glad when I pay her so she'll *shut up*."

"Okay. Let's start over. How's your leg?"

"*Which* leg?"

"Your *left* leg. The *polio* leg. Just the one that's given you trouble for fifteen years. That's *which leg*."

"Polio. Polio? The only person I know with polio is Noni's friend Frances, in Alabama."

"Does the year 1954 ring a bell?" I asked.

"Yeah. That was the first time we spent the *whole* summer in Alabama. Mom and Dad sure fooled us the *second* time, didn't they? Hi. Welcome back from vacation, kids. Welcome to your new broken homes."

"They should have divorced *long* before they did. They would have made themselves *and* a lot of people happier."

"No," she said. "They just never should have left backwoods Alabama and come to the Big City. *All* those glittering objects. *All* that excitement."

"Are we talking about the same town *here?*" I asked.

"Towns are as big as your capacity for wonder, as Fitzgerald said," said Ethel.

"Okay. Back to weird. Are you sure you never had polio when you were a kid? That you haven't *been* in North Carolina the last month at some weird science place? That you weren't causing me to hallucinate being a time-traveler?"

"Franklin," she said. "I have never seen it, but I *do* believe you are drunk. Why don't you hang up now and call me back when you are sober. I still love you, but I will not tolerate a drunken brother calling me while I am trying to sleep.

"Good-bye now—"

"Wait! *Wait!* I want to know, are my travels through? Can I get back to my real life now?"

"How would I know?" asked Ethel. "I'm not the King Of Where-You-Go."

"Maybe. Maybe not."

"Go sober up now. Next time call me at work. Nights."

She hung up.

And then I thought: what would it be like to watch everyone slow down; the clock start whirling clockwise around the dial til it turned gray like it was full of dishwater, and then suddenly be out at the spaceport they're going to build out at the edge of town and watch the Mars rocket take off every Tuesday?

And: I would never know the thrill of standing, with a satchel full of comics under my arm, waiting at the end of Eve Arden's driveway for her to get home from the studio . . .

Afterword
The King of Where-I-Go

This was the companion-piece to "Horse of a Different Color" written under the same circumstances, and with the same publishing history.

This was done in 2005, before the hospitalization, and I found myself living some of it out for the two months I stayed with my sister in Mississippi in 2008.

People as me: "Did your sister have polio, like in the story?"

Well, no. The polio survivor was my late Aunt Ethel, who got polio when she was four, and lived to be eighty-six years old. I extrapolated (that's writer-talk for made up) the rest of it.

A lot of the story touches on the dark underside of American Cold War research, by people knowing, and unknowing.

Stories of the KGB and CIA with great serried rankes of psychics, trying to give Kruschev or Ike heart attacks, trying to panic NATO or Warsaw Pact troops into dropping their guns and running. Ot trying to will the radioactive elements from atomic bombs . . .

All this in a nice story about a brother and sister going through a bad patch.

You have to watch every minute.

This is the last thing of mine that was up for a Hugo.

"The Bravest Girl I Ever Knew . . ."

From *Movie Fan Magazine,* April 1952:

A NOTE FROM MOVIE FAN'S EDITOR:
Everybody knows the story, or thinks they do. The most famous find in movie history, before Lana Turner's discovery at Schrafft's drustore. A movie producer, desperate for a leading lady, finds exactly the right girl stealing apples from a vendor at the height of the Depression—seven months later she's the most famous woman in the world.

Her career blazed across the screen for exactly one year—then, like the later Louise Brooks—she left, with no regrets; the usual wisdom is life and Hollywood broke her heart.

But the story is not that simple (Hollywood stories never are) and for the first time, we at the *Movie Fan* are going to set the record straight, removing all the glamour and tinsel. The true story is both more normal and much stranger than all legend and fiction written about her. Miss Ellencamp has spent the last year assiduously combing through studio records, newspaper articles, and publicity handouts; a truly huge mass of materials, building a true picture of the meteoric star; a piece we call simply:

ANN
By Margot Luisa Ellencamp

First off, she was Canadian, born in the community of Dollerton on Vancouver Bay in 1910. Her father, "Big" Bill Darrow, formerly a logger, was killed with half his battalion at Beaumont-Hamel; her mother, Angelina, was taken off by the Spanish Influenza epidemic in 1919.

Secondly (as those who've seen her last two films know), she was brunette. For her first and most famous role, the producer Carl Denham insisted she be blonde, to play up the dark vs. light, Beauty and the Beast theme. (She and Charley the cook spent much of the voyage to Skull Island getting exactly the right shade of blonde, and the right amount of curl with the many home-permanent formulas, still in their infancy, that Denham had picked up in a beauty-shop supply store on the way back to the ship, once he had his leading lady, just before they sailed.)

Third, as those who've seen all three films know, she could do more than just scream—even in Denham's Kong she does a lot more than that—it's just the screaming that most people remember.

When Denham asked her "Did you ever do any acting?" she said "Extra work out on Long Island—the studio's closed now." Well, that was Paramount; at the time the movie was set, the Astoria studio had just suffered a disastrous fire and the decision had been made to move all production to the West Coast.

That ended Paramount's ability to do something the other studios couldn't—to use Broadway talent without them having to take the five-day train trip west and live in California while making their films.

The "extra work" Ann Darrow had done had been in several of those: the Four Marx Brothers had made both *Cocoanuts* and *Animal Crackers* at Paramount's Astoria studio in the daytime while appearing in *I'll Say She Is!* at night. (It ran on Broadway for two years.) If you look closely (as I did) you can see that Ann is one of the crowd of girls on the beach just before the Irving Berlin "Monkey-Doodle-Do" musical number in *Cocoanuts,* and is one of the guests at the unveiling of the painting in *Animal Crackers.* She was 19 and 20 when she did those. She's only on for a few seconds in each, and don't be looking for a blonde.

Like all Hollywood stories, even her extra work has been glamorized and embellished—stories circulated that three of the four brothers were so smitten by her beauty, they tried various campaigns and stratagems to lure her into love affairs.[1] Most writers think this was a figment of some publicist's imagination, retroactively fired by the thoughts of Ann's beauty and the Marx's notorious behavior.

The Depression hit Ann as hard as it did anyone else; she'd had a few walk-on parts in a couple of revues written by writer friends of hers, but those jobs, like the extra-work, dried up. At the time Denham found her, she was living in a $6.00 a week rooming house at the edge of the Village, and, according to friends, having to borrow part of that most weeks.

Then Denham offered her the "fame and adventure and the thrill of a lifetime, and the long sea voyage leaving at six o'clock in the morning" and the rest is just like Kong; little known is that

---

1 But of what single woman on a Marx Bros'. movie set was this not true (with the possible exception of Margaret Dumont)? The best quote was Archie Lee Johnson's "In the movies, Harpo acted out his libido: on movie sets, Chico acted on his libido."

all the scenes in *Kong* detailing Ann and Jack's adventures from the time Driscoll left Denham on the other side of the ravine were recreations—about the last thing Denham still had money for after Kong fell off the building—he saw the movie as a way to recoup some of his losses from the disaster that was Kong as a Broadway attraction.

What was recreated for the film were the early fight with the Tyrannosaurus, the scenes of Kong with Ann in his lair, the scenes of Jack and Ann's escape from Kong, and a few of the scenes of Kong breaking the gate in the wall to get at the native village, in his search for Ann.[2]

The rest was pieced together from scenes taken aboard ship and on Skull Island, and newsreels and Denham's own films of Kong as a exhibition and of his New York rampage.

In the studio, they got a well-known animator to recreate scenes; the effects were so wonderful and lifelike it was hard to tell where the real Kong left off and the 18" actor-model took his place. But the effects were hurried, which accounts for Kong's variation in size. Assume when you see Kong, that everything when the camera in not near Denham is a recreation done in the few weeks between the death of the real Kong in March, and the release of the movie in June.

---

2 True to Denham's prediction, the cameraman ran. After filming Kong shaking the sailors off the log, and getting that horrifying pan-shot down into the ravine, the cameraman went with Denham back to the Wall. Denham was filming while Kong was trying to break the gate, then went to help in the futile attempt to stop Kong from breaking through. The guy dropped the camera and bolted for the shore; Denham shot most of the destruction of the village. The cameraman, now by the boats, got the shots of Kong's gassing.

What mattered to Ann was that she and Jack Driscoll, the man she loved, worked together in the studio a few weeks, filling in the gaps in the story.

Kong as a living exhibit premiered two days before FDR took office as president, and it made an enormous amount of money that first night, even though FDR had already announced the four-day Bank Holiday in which all banks throughout the nation would be closed. People turned out to see *Kong* at top ticket prices, no matter what.

The same thing happened when the film came out—it was an enormous hit. Denham had been right all along about "being a millionaire and sharing it with you, boys" and in this case, girl—or it would have been true had not Denham's expenses and litigations not eaten up all the money from the exhibition and the movie.

But by the time the movie premiered, Denham and Englehorn were on their way back to Skull Island, to find the treasure that would eventually save Denham, and with another leading lady.

The people ask why didn't he just take Ann back with him? At the time of his greatest financial troubles, the one valuable asset he did have was Ann Darrow's personal contract. She was the most famous woman and actress in the world at the time. Denham had loaned her out to MGM for a huge sum of money for ther next super production.

Of course she did it—she owed everything to Carl Denham—but little did she realize she would have to do it with a sorrowing and broken heart.

She and Jack were married two weeks after the premier of *Kong,* the movie. It was a heady time in America, and everyone knew Prohibition was going to end. So one night while Ann was off making a personal appearance at a charity event, Jack ran into a bunch of sailors he'd shipped with before he became Captain Englehorn's first mate, and they went off to some speakeasy and drank some poison liquor. Four of the sailors died, Jack among them.

The newspapers that week said she was inconsolable—first Denham and the ship gone back to the Island; her on loan-out to MGM and now Jack dead. That was the state of things when she took the Zephyr out to California in the summer of 1933, to star in *The Return of Tarzan,* where she played Queen La of Opar, opposite Johnny Weissmuller and Maureen O'Sullivan back in their roles from *Tarzan, The Ape Man* of 1932.

Some of her heart is still up there on the screen—especially in the scenes of longing for Tarzan. "It was La and Tarzan before this woman came. We were happy. Let us be happy again. Rule with me, over my kingdom!" Cedric Gibbons' set design for the collapsed Opar (the Ophir of the Bible)—the half-broken dome, remnants of former buildings, ruined gardens, crumbled and vine-covered statues—all got across a feeling of a vanished civilization, older and larger than the one on Skull Island. The inhabitants—La's subjects—shambling half-ape men, beautiful women—chanted and danced at the thought their Queen was to marry the Lord of the Jungle.

Ann threw herself into her work, all the while fending off Weissmuller's "busy, busy hands" as she called them once in an interview ("he was like a six-foot upright octopus," she said). Her screen time in the film is 30 of the 96 minutes, but they were memorable and intense ones. The famous still of her (not in the movie) half-crouched on her throne, backed by the two crossed 20-foot-long ivory tusks, still sells for high prices to collectors of movie memorabilia. More so even than the Elephant's Graveyard sequence in the first movie, what most people remember is the scene with La and Tarzan standing on the broken balcony, looking over the vine-covered remnants of the former great city while the Moon rises behind the two bodiless legs (broken off just at hip level) of the statue of the Ape-god of the ruined city. (Cedric Gibbons again . . .)

MGM rushed her into her next (and what proved to be last) film; it's her most atypical, and the one she liked best. It was in the middle of filming *Take My Heart—Please* that the first news came out of the Indian Ocean that Denham was on his way back.

Ann Darrow got the role of a lifetime (and the cast of a lifetime to act with) in *Take My Heart—Please.* During the filming of the offbeat movie, some publicist had put up a sign, supposedly from her, on her dressing-room door (please—no more gorillas)—it sounds like publicity, as Ann never denigrated Kong's role in her life in any published interview.

In the movie Ann is a low-tier stage actress who lives in a rooming-house much like the ones she'd lived in only eighteen months before—she and her best friend Zuxxy—("the Xs are silent"), are hired by a producer to play (offstage) the parts of the producer's and assistant producer's wives. This is in order to counteract the suspicions of the society mother of a rising starlet about bachelor producers of Broadway shows. (They want the starlet in their next play.)

The usual complications ensue; one screwy complication leads to the lies that set up the next one; Anne's character and Zuxxy end up with the (wrong) right people; there's a tremendous chase with the hook-and-ladder fire truck and a trolley-car.

For Zuxxy, Eve Arden was on loan-out from Paramount (in return, Loretta Young spent two weeks at Paramount in a South Sea movie no one ever saw). The producer was played by Leon Ames, the associate producer by Franchot Tone, who ends up with Ann's character while Arden ends up with Ames; the society dame by Maragret Dumont—this time in a not-very-comic role, and she was very good in it. There are bits by Edgar Kennedy, Raymond

Walburn, and Franklin Pangborn; Grady Sutton is the young starlet's brother, sort of a thinking man's suspicious weasel—the more he looks, the more he sees about the false situation.

It had the only screenplay ever worked on at one time or another by the young John Huston, the not-so-young F. Scott Fitzgerald, and Dorothy Parker and her husband Alan Campbell.

People who saw it at the time, or in re-release, think it's a wonderful film, full of the kinds of things people used to go to the movies for. Ann was never better; she's a terrific physical comedienne, and the playing between her and Eve Arden is just magic.

It was one of only twelve films MGM released that year that only broke even at the box office. No one knows why—it's a much better movie than 90% of the hits the studio had that year. In December, just after *The Return of Tarzan* was released, she got a telegram from Hawaii.

> GEE KID LOOKS LIKE YOURE A HIT. WILL CATCH THE FLICK IN HONOLULU TOMORROW. RETURNING TO THE STATES NEXT WEEK. DON'T WORRY ABOUT ME—THINGS ARE GREAT OUR MONEY WORRIES ARE OVER. STAY THE WAY YOU ARE AND BE SWELL.
>
> DENHAM

It was with much surprise that Ann was given the 1934 Academy Award for Best Supporting Actress, in a strong field, for her role in *The Return of Tarzan.* (Gibbons won the first-ever-given one for his Art Direction) At the ceremony, Eve Arden had a telegram from her that said

EVE IF I WIN JUST SAY THANK YOU VERY MUCH AND SIT DOWN.

So Eve said, "Thank you very much and sit down."

That same month, *Take My Heart—Please* opened to some great reviews and disappointing box office.

By then, Ann was 6000 miles away.

From the only interview Paul Young[3] ever gave (in 1941), to an AP stringer who had walked the 50 miles from the nearest railroad station in the hopes of getting a story from him.

PY: I fell in love with that girl the first time I laid eyes on her. Not the googly-eyed movie love, either. I said, "Paul, this is the one for you." That was late in '33, and I was leaving this rubber-and-peanut plantation for the States on business anyway, and I set about winning her heart, after all that Kong stuff, and the sad business about Driscoll, and Denham's troubles and whatnot. (I once said: No One has to worry about Carl Denham . . .)

Anyway, I knew people who knew people, and I found myself at a party somewhere up in the LA Hills and there she was, and brother, I wasn't the least bit disappointed. I had shaved off my mustache for the trip: she was shorter than she looked onscreen, and she reached up and fingered the dip under my nose and asked, "How do you shave in there?" and I said something Hollywood, with embarrassment, like 'For you, I'll cover it back up' or something.

Three months later we were on our way back here, as happily married as two people have ever been in the history of the world.

---

3 Despite what some sources state: he was not, nor related to, the famous bamboo fly rod maker of the same name and era.

FROM: *The Ninth Wonder of This World! My Life,* by Carl Denham, 1946.

She came into my office after she finished that last picture. She looked around eyeing all the sharp new stuff I had.

"It's true, then," she said. "I don't have to worry for you any more, do I, Mr. Denham?" (She never called me anything but Mr. Denham in all the time I knew her.)

"Don't worry about me ever again, Ann," I said. "I'm rolling in it. Anything you need? Anything at all! You don't know how much it meant to me, those first few destitute months on the way back to Skull Island, knowing you were here, giving it your all, becoming a star."

"Well, yes, there is one thing," she said. "I've fallen in love with a wonderful man—he's, he's not like Jack at all—but there's no fakery about him, either. He wants me to be his wife."

"That's just great, Ann," I said. "If you're sure that's what you want."

"I'm as sure of it as I've ever been about anything." And she reached across my desk and took my hand—the only time she ever did that, either. "It's what I want. I want to ask you to release me from my contract. My future husband will pay whatever amount you think—"

"Pay? Pay! There's not enough money in the whole wide world to pay what your contract's worth, kid." I said.

She looked crestfallen.

I reached in my desk and took out her personal contract, signed like what seemed long ages ago on a rusty old ship. I tore it in half and handed her both pieces.

"This isn't something you buy and sell. This is something you give away for love." Then I slapped myself in the face. "What am I saying? The price for this is you two owe me a dinner so I can meet this guy who's taking you away from all this. I want to size him up."

"You name it," she said. "We'd love to."

"Tonight. The Coconut Grove. 8 sharp."

"We'll be there."

And then she leaned over and kissed me on the forehead.

"I've always wanted to do that," she said, and tousled my thinning locks. "That, too."

"Banana oil!" I said. "Get outta here before I change my mind!"

She left.

That night as I said good-bye to them outside the club, I thought sure she would be okay for the rest of her life (well, she was, but you know what I mean.) I shook hands with Paul—working hands, not the ones of a sissy—"Take care of my little girl. I mean it."

"I surely will," he said. "I love her more than anything. I'm the luckiest guy in the world."

"If I had a heart," I said, "I would probably love her, too."

They got in the cab and waved. They looked so happy.

It was the last time I saw her alive.

Poor kid.

From the 1941 interview with Paul Young:

PY: I asked her when we first got back here if she didn't miss all that.

"Not really," she said. "Though sometimes I think what a wonderful thing it would have been to make more movies with Eve. She's just so great.

"But look around, Paul. It's just like you said—it's cool at night, and not as hot and muggy as somebody would think. The world can go by out there somewhere, and you'd never even know it was there."

She loved this place. It was like my whole life led me to buy this plantation, just so it would be there for her when she needed it. It made me proud to have done that. That had been the major accomplishment of my life.

FROM: *The Ninth Wonder of This World! My Life,* by Carl Denham, 1946. I wrote her a letter about a year later. I put it in here to show that I was still thinking at the time . . .

April 20, 1935

Dear Ann (and Paul),
I can't believe it's been a year—I've been so busy I just looked up and a whole year was gone. I got to see your last picture a few months ago—you and it were swell; so was everybody else in it, and you're right—that Eve Arden is a pistol! Sorry the picture tanked. But it's still there for everybody to see, from now 'til the end of time. They can't take that away from you.

What with the two pictures I made this year, and what's left of the Skull Island treasure, I look to be sitting pretty for a long long time—but I've got to admit, I'm getting a little too stiff to be running around jungles and throwing gas bombs and such.

People keep bringing me plays and movie scripts they say you'd be great in, and trying to get me to get you back over here, but I tell them, "Don't get your boxers in a twist—I know she's happy AND she knows the door's always open if she ever changes her mind. Meanwhile, write your stuff for Carole Lombard and Jean Arthur—though neither has Ann's range."

I just want to say again how much knowing you has meant to me—we gave 'em some socko stuff, didn't we, kid? I hope you're tremendously happy, and my best to Paul.

Your Pal,
Carl Denham

From the Paul Young interview:

PY: She woke me up the night of the day we'd gotten back from Madoni, where she'd seen the doctor and knew she was going to have a baby. She was upset.

"For the first time in a year," she said. "I dreamed about Kong, and it wasn't a nightmare, like all the other times in the past. We were on top of Skull Mountain, outside the cave where the pterodactyl picked me up. But the only ones in the sky were far, far away. Kong was sitting, leaning forward, his hands out in front of him, his legs dangling over the abyss. We were just sitting. I didn't say anything. It was like he knew what was going to happen. Like Denham said—was a tough egg, but he'd already cracked up and gone sappy. Like he'd already accepted anything and everything that was going to happen. Because of me.

"Paul, no matter what the future holds, I want you to know it's—well, it's not necessarily for the best, always, but it will be what's supposed to happen. I'll be okay if I know you're going to do one of two things for me. If I have a boy, I want you to name him—don't be upset, please—Jack Denham Young and give him this"—she'd been shopping in Madoni, where there's not very much shopping to be had, but they'd just got in stuff from Nairobi—where it came from in British-controlled Africa I don't know—she handed me a baseball glove—"I know there aren't any teams out here, but teach him how to play like he was a boy in America."

"Ann," I asked. "Why are you talking like this? You can teach him how to play. You've got a better arm than me!"

"—and if it's a girl," she said, and handed me a crazy-looking doll"—I want you to name her Jill Eve Young and give her this, whose name, I just decided, is Genevive. Can you promise me you'll do those things?"

"Of course!" I said. "Of course. But don't be talking like this. You're going to be fine. We'll have as many kids as you want; we'll make our own baseball team."

She put her finger up to my lip. I'd grown my mustache back by then.

"Just do whichever of those things you need to do, and I'll be happy. Well, happier. Dreaming of Kong that way made me realize the world goes on forever."

"Well, sure it does." I said. Then she went back to sleep, and I remember just standing there watching over her for a long time.

That was six years ago (this interview was from 1941). There isn't an hour that goes by that I don't think about her and miss her. (I'll take you out to her grave when you're through interviewing me.) But of course I have Jill there to remember her—look at them playing . . . I don't think Joe's got all his growth yet—he's going to be a real handful before he gets through.

I just wish Ann would be here to see all of this. Sometimes I'm sorry I ever brought her here, but then again, I wouldn't trade what we had for anything. Sometimes I think she was just visiting us here on Earth, and her life was like a dream, rounded with a gorilla on each end.

You want to come down by the river with me now? It's really very peaceful there.

It was her favorite spot.

Afterword "The Bravest Girl I Ever Knew . . ."

"BEING CAREFUL WHAT YOU WISH FOR: A PART OF THE TRUE AND TERRIBLE HISTORY OF SF, Or: Why You're Reading in the All-Original Polyphony *a story that was printed Somewhere Else First.*[4]

It all happened back in the long-lost year of 2005, because I was venting to Paul Di Filippo.

He'd just (as is his wont) sent me a copy of the newest thing he was in, with a story called "The Mysterious Iowans." The book was *The Mammoth Book of New Jules Verne Adventures,* edited by Mike Ashley and Eric Brown.

"Where'd *this* come from?" I wrote. "I never *heard* of this anthology. Why wasn't *I* asked be in *this* anthology? Steven Utley *didn't* write a story thirty-five years ago that *should* be in *this* book!"

I reached my apogee. "I used to be asked to be in *everything!* People haven't asked me to be in stuff *for years!*"

---

4 This afterword was written for the anthology *Polyphony* 7, which was cancelled before publication.

Well, I knew the answers to *that* myself. A) For a while there editors were asking me to be in the *stupidest-sounding* theme anthologies I'd *ever* heard of, stuff I wouldn't get near in a million years; stuff so far from what I wrote I was sure they had mistaken me for some other hack. Or, B) They had a deadline so close there was No Way I could do anything for it. See, unless it's something I've ALREADY been thinking about, I need six to eight months or so just to figure out WHAT I want to do.

So A) and B) got polite notes saying NO. I guess editors got tired of asking.

Well, Paul must have been feeling goosey that day, or something, or he may have mistaken my tirade against *the field* for having something to do with *him.* Or something. What I think happened is that he passed the word on to Karen Haber.

Karen wrote me inviting me in to *Kong Unbound,* one of the two *King Kong*-themed anthologies that year that were to be published in time for Peter Jackson's remake of *King Kong,* which was to premier in December 2005.

As soon as she invited me, I *knew exactly* what I was going to write, and I knew *how* to do it, right off the bat. Happens about three times a career.

"Sure thing, Toots," I wrote back.

That was late April. In May, I had to be in Taos Ski Valley, New Mexico, as the Wandering Scholar for the second year at the peer-group Rio Hondo Writers' Workshop run by Walter Jon Williams.

I stopped off at George R. R. Martin's house in Santa Fe after a seventeen-straight-hour drive from Austin. (I'm an *old man,* and seventeen-hour drives aren't the snap they used to be when I was eighteen.) George and I have been friends since 1963, when we wrote letters to each other *so long* it took *four cents* to mail them, he from junior high in Bayonne, New Jersey, and me from 10th grade in Arlington, Texas. A lot of blood has flown under the bridge since then. Anyway, this was Friday night—I had to be in Taos Ski Valley at noon on Sunday. George, Parris, and I had a rollicking dinner (I was rummy-dummy from the drive). Then I went over to sleep in George's office-house, the one across the street.

Saturday morning I rolled out of bed, drank two pots of coffee like Popeye eating spinach, flopped myself down in a papa-san chair and wrote "The Bravest Girl I Ever Knew." Saturday pm I typed it up on my Adler manual portable typewriter and went in while George was clicking away on whatever *goddamn doorstop* of a *Songs* novel he was finishing that year, and xeroxed enough copies of the story for the workshop. (If I remembered correctly, there was only one shop with a copier in Taos Ski Valley in the summer, and it was a quarter a pop . . . *not* the place to do copies for a fifteen-person workshop of your fourteen-page story.)

Anyway, I drive ninety miles to the workshop on Sunday. Monday morning I take the original of the mss the mile straight up the hill under the ski lift to what passes for the post office in the summer, and mail it off to Karen.

Thereby *dooming* the story, for reasons that will quickly become apparent (and having nothing to do with Karen, who was a champ through this *whole* ordeal).

Of course when I got back to Austin nine days later there was an acceptance from Karen waiting. She said the contracts would be on the way soon. "Say hi to Bob" I said in my letter back. (That would be Robert Silverberg, her husband.) (This will be important later.)

Well, along about early June (I think) I get this contract. It's *not* from Karen. It's *not* from Simon & Shuster, the publisher of

Kong Unbound. It's from Byron Preiss Visual Publications, BPVP for short, who was acting as packager for the book. (I *had not known* this: I wrote the story for Karen.)

For thirty-five years I had avoided dealing with BPVP. Once again, I was the square peg in the round hole. First, "The Bravest Girl I Ever Knew" was fiction. *Everything else* in the book is nonfiction, including swell pieces by Jack Williamson, Silverberg, Di Filippo, and a bunch of others. The contract is set up for nonfiction, so half the clauses don't apply to the story. There are restrictive clauses, no mention of grants of rights for inclusion in single-author short-story collections, *Best of the Year,* or awards volumes, which are pretty standard throughout the business. There's twelve month's exclusivity, and electronic and worldwide rights, etc. It was the worst contract for a piece of fiction I'd ever seen in my (then) thirty-six years in the business.

I called Karen. "I can't sign this," I say.

"Cross out the stuff that bothers you," she says.

"Then I can sign this," I say. I fix it up and send it off.

A week later I get a phone call. It's BPVP. "Who told *you* you could *change* the contract?" they ask. "Karen," I say. "You know, *The Editor?*"

"Well, she *shouldn't* have told you you *could* change it. Everybody has to sign the same contract. Or we can't pay anybody, *or* take the book."

"Mine's a piece of fiction," I say. "That's not what *this* contract is set up for."

"*Sign the contract* like we sent it to you."

I went to the office and found a clean copy of the contract before I'd diddled with it. I made three copies and signed them. Then I wrote the naughtiest letter I've ever written to someone where money's coming from, i.e., Byron Preiss himself, telling him what I thought of his contracts and his business dealings, I xeroxed that, too, and sent the letter and contracts off to him.

Of course, all this arrived at the office the day Byron Preiss was killed in a car wreck out on Long Island.

Nobody at the office wanted to deal with me, *or* my letter. So they asked Karen to call me and find out what was the matter.

I told her.

"Well, I can see why you're upset. I would be, too, if it were my story."

"Thanks," I said. "Let me know how things are going, now that I've *signed* the damn thing."

That was June. July and August go by. No money. I figure it's more BPVP bullshit. But no—or at least not *officially*—Karen sends out emails to everybody else and a letter to me.

The problem is Peter Jackson. He hasn't signed off yet on the merchandising rights to *King Kong.*

In our case, i.e., *Kong Unbound,* the merchandising rights *in toto* consist of a scene from the new movie on the cover, since all the other essays and my story are about either the 1933 or the 1976 versions of the film (in August 2005 *no one* had seen the *new* movie yet).

The way I understand it, Peter Jackson, who's just been paid $200 million for *The Lord of the Rings* (and is going to sue for *another* $100 million, because the studio was dumb enough to *give him* the figures they worked from, and his accountants said, "They owe you another 100 million simoleons *if* those figures are right."). Anyway, this guy has not signed off on the merchandising rights and is keeping all of us from getting *our* American simoleons. (I'm sure my not getting my three hundred dollars was not keeping him tossing and turning at night.) Not really *his* fault, either, as he was in post-production on *Kong* eight thousand miles away.

Anyway, September-October-November pass. I hear (by rumor) Jackson has *finally* signed off on the rights, and the flood of merchandise begins. The movie *is* coming out in December (Lawrence Person and I will in fact review it for Locusmag.com).

On December 1, 2005, I receive a *Media Mail* package from BPVP. It was mailed *sixteen days ago.* Inside are two copies of *Kong Unbound* and a check for three hundred dollars. *Media Mail,* after all these months.

I call Karen. Bob answers. "Got your money yet?" I ask.

"No. Even though Karen got paid for editing the book last week."

"And they didn't notice *your* address was the same as *hers?*"

"No, they didn't."

"Don't get excited, Bob," I said. "It's coming *Media Mail, with* the books."

There was silence on the line a few seconds.

Then Bob said: "Don't you *love it* when they do *that?*"

"Mine took sixteen days from NYC. Yours can't be more than a few days behind that."

I rang off.

Besides those two copies I got that December day in 2005, I have seen exactly one copy for sale, in a Borders, two weeks later.

Then, on a day in early spring 2006, BPVP declared bankruptcy for themselves, including I-Books, after lying to everyone about the state of their upcoming projects, and everything has been tied up in a neverending bankruptcy procedure ever since. It never got down to intellectual property—*mine anyway*—and someone bought the whole shebang and is *still* trying to figure stuff out.

BPVP and Simon & Shuster's exclusivity on my story ended in December 2006.

As for your publisher's reason she wants to put out the Only Story you'll ever see as a reprint in *Polyphony,* she said: "Nobody saw it."

And she was right.

Here it is, another refugee of the True and Terrible History of SF Malzberg's always going on and on about.

And he's right, too.

Thin, On the Ground

There's a sampler on Gramma Elkins' wall that says: "You don't have to look for Trouble: It's looking for you."—Uncle Breck

Of course, they tell me he always also said: "If unarmed and assaulted, pull a tree out of the ground and flail away."

We weren't looking for trouble. We were going to Mexico to celebrate graduation from high school, class of 1962.

I was the third person in my family to make it *all the way* through school. *We* were me and Bobby Mitchell, my absolute best friend since 1st grade. We got in the 1953 Ford pickup we owned together, way before dawn of the morning after we graduated; it was so early the big comet everyone was talking about was blazing across the sky.

Bobby, who's a lot smarter than me, said it was called Comet 1962 IIB and had a Norwegian and a Japanese guy's names after it.

I just thought it was big and pretty.

We drove off under it, heading south. The stoplight on the highway was still on blink.

—

We'd bought the truck back in January, and we'd stood in line like everyone else in Texas, at the courthouse over in Crosley, on April 1st to get our new black-number-on-white-background plates to replace the 1961 white-on-black plates: and then we'd flipped a nickel and called it and Bobby had slept in the truck down at the service station the night of April 14th to be in line to get a new inspection sticker, which everyone had to have on April 15th. We were new to truck ownership, but we knew there was a better way to do it than *that* . . .

That was all behind us, and we were heading south. On our dashboard was a glow-in-the-dark Jesus Bobby's sister had won in Sunday school, way back in the third grade, for reciting *all* the books of the Bible, pretty much in one breath. When we bought the truck, Bobby convinced her to sell us the statue for a whole dollar. She didn't want to sell it, she kept it on top of her chest-of-drawers in her bedroom. "*We* can drive it all over the world," he said. "What are *you* gonna do, take your dresser out for a drive?"

Bobby was looking at the plastic Jesus. He started singing:

"My name is Jesus, the son of Joe:

Hello-hello-hello . . ."

And kept singing it as we passed through Rising Star as the east was beginning to lighten.

We'd left home before sunup, and we pulled up at the parking lot at the bordertown (it was called Bordertown, Texas) at 6 p.m. on a blazing hot May day. Even from here, you could hear the sounds of Tex-Mex music coming across the Rio Grande, which was about 40 feet wide here.

"Not so *grande*," said Bobby, who spoke some Spanish.

We walked across the wooden bridge, and a vista opened up before us—a whole town of one-story buildings spread out before us as fas as the eye could see—the only thing taller was a miniature Eiffel-tower-looking thing with an umbrella and chair on top and a man asleep in it.

The ever-alert fire lookout," said Bobby. The *bomberos*—firemen."

We nodded at the Mexican border guards. They waved back. "Keep out of *real* trouble," said a dapper-looking one to us in English.

The bridge emptied onto what looked like the main street. There was a big sign just as you came to it: Official Exchange Rate Today (and a space for a chalked message which today said) $1.00 US = 12 Pesos.

"Think of everything as 8 cents," said Bobby. "If it's too expensive at 8 cents, it's too expensive in pesos."

Guys, like carnival barkers, were lined up in front of all the shops, which looked like used record stores to me. "Bargains galore!" they yelled. "No down payment to GI Joe!" they said to a couple of soldiers. "Your uniform is your collateral!" I wondered what the hell they could be selling in *installments.* "Shopper's Paradise; a consumer's Eden!" yelled another.

We came to a store. There was a guy standing in front of it like the others, but with his arms crossed and not saying anything.

As we got to him he said, "Please come in and buy some junk so I can close early."

Well, *honesty* is the best policy.

We got a gold-plated machete and a red-and-white striped *rebozo* and a two-gallon purple piggy-bank with a comical expression on its face. The bank was covered with painted green and orange flowers.

"Where's Boy's Town?" asked Bobby.

"This *whole* town's Boy's Town," said the man, "but the second street to the left"—he pointed—"is what *you* want."

"Do you have a sack for this stuff?"

"Here's how we do it." He put the machete and piggy-bank inside the *rebozo,* made a couple of folds, and handed the neat package, square and tight, by the rebozo-hood handle, to Bobby.

"Could you do that *again*?" asked Bobby, his eyes wide.

"No, I cannot," said the shopkeeper. "I can only make a package that neat once a day. Your pardon."

As we left the shop he was putting up the Closed sign on the door. We heard the wire security gate scraping down behind us.

Imagine an endless honky-tonk. The street looked like the inside of a juke-box—colored lights, noise and music everywhere, neon beginning to come on, and more guys yelling. The blinking lights said "Girls! Girls!! Girls!!!" And "30 Lovely Señoritas—18 Beautiful Costumes!" and "*This is* the place!"

It was starting to get dark, and the outline of the comet appeared with the first stars. Bobby said tonight was going to be about the brightest it would get, and it would fade over the next month or two.

A guy came toward us, singing:

> *"Me nombre Jésus, hijo de José*
> *Hola-hola-hola"*

He passed us by, a broad grin on his face. A crowd of guys and soldiers headed down the street. We started to join them.

Then I thought I heard crying. I looked over a couple of streets, and a woman was walking away toward the river. The sound was coming from her, and it was the most heart-wrenching thing I'd ever heard.

"Hey!" I said. "That lady's in *trouble*."

Bobby held up his rebozo-package like a shield. "It's probably a scam. We go help her and we get jumped."

"That's *real* crying," I said. "That's not fake."

We hurried to help her.

She had gone out onto the river shore. She was wearing a long black dress and a thing like Little-Red-Riding-Hood, only in the fading light it looked blue. Her crying rose in pitch and force.

I saw that there were two kids on the Texas side, and they were holding their arms out toward her.

A guy with a fishing pole was coming up the riverbank toward us on our side. He stopped and dropped the pole and a couple of Rio Grande perch he had on a stringer.

"*Caramba!*" he yelled. "*La Llorena!*" and ran away.

The woman's crying never stopped. The kids were crying, too, holding out their hands.

The woman turned toward us. Inside the hood was the head of a horse.

When we stopped running we were in front of a place called Salon de Baile.

"You look like you've seen a ghost," said the guy out front.

"Don't ask," said Bobby.

It was a real dance hall with a *conjunto* band and actual couples dancing, and a stag-line, and on the other side of the room, women waiting to be asked to dance.

Hey. This place is *legit*," said Bobby. "There are two *duennas* with the women."

"What a let down," I said.

Bobby ordered two beers from the waiter. We drank them in a few seconds. I was still breathing hard from the run from the river.

We watched the couples dance. They were dressed for a Saturday night (which is what it was) in their finest. There were even one or two guys in *vaquero* outfits, the full thing; one guy who was dancing had on a powder-blue outfit with silver trim and back at the table he'd come from was a big blue and silver sombrero across the back of a chair,

"It's *different* here," I said to Bobby. "A guy can go out on a Saturday night in a powder-blue suit."

The band played faster and the dancers swirled around.

Then there was a scream, and a woman collapsed and everyone ran to her. They stirred the air near her with their fans and their *mantillas*. She screamed from the floor.

"*El hombre pie de gallo!* she yelled. "*El hombre pie . . .*"

Bobby went over to listen. He came back.

"She was dancing with the guy in the blue suit," he said. "*Muy sauvacito* as she described him, very dapper. She was *really* dancing with the music; she looked down, and instead of boots, he had the feet of a rooster. A sign of the devil."

I looked over. The guy in the blue and silver outfit was gone, and so was his hat. I hadn't seen anyone leave.

"Let's go *somewhere else*," I said.

We were outside. The comet was so bright it lit the place up like there was a full moon, though I knew that wouldn't be until the middle of next month.

A wagon rolled down the street. It was the first wagon I'd seen in years, drawn by two mules. One had a child's sombrero on its head, with holes cut out for its ears. I saw it from the neon lights of the joint next door.

There was a woman standing outside, smoking a cigarette. A guy on a horse rode up, big sombrero, silver studs sparkling off the saddle from the strings of colored lights in the street.

He asked for a light; he held a *cigarillo* down toward her.

She looked up. She dropped the Zippo she'd taken out of her handbag and began to scream: *Aaiiee! Aaiiee!*

A guy came out of the bar, stopped, and yelled: "*Caracoles! El jinte sin cabeza!*" And ran off. So did the woman.

I looked up. Between the collar of the horseman's jacket and the brim of his hat, I could see the top of a tree three blocks away, silver in the comet's light.

The guy shrugged his shoulders, turned his horse around and went off down the way. I watched the scenery through his invisible head. He turned left two streets down.

We ran into the bar.

It was very late. We were drunk. The street had about four or five people on it. The barkers had all gone inside, and some of the colored lights and neon signs had been turned off. If I weren't so drunk, it would have looked sad.

We made our way as best we could down the street. The comet blazed away, taking up half the sky.

"This stuff's getting heavy," said Bobby. "Take it for a while." He handed me the wrapped-up *rebozo*.

He was right. It was heavy.

We were looking for a place with nothing but red lights out front. We came to the corner of a cross-street.

There was a well-dressed man standing in the diagonal corner; formal wear, shiny cufflinks, cummerbund, and all. Another guy was walking toward him on the side-street, whistling. There was some conversation between them—the walking man slowed and answered as he neared.

I'll swear the comet-light brightened then dimmed then brightened again *by a half*. I looked up, then back. Where the formally dressed man had been was a seedier-looking individual. His clothes had changed, his hair was wilder, he looked like a gargoyle Betty Boop; his head was as wide as his shoulders. There was a thing like a butterfly's tongue under his chin, and it uncurled like an elephant's trunk and went up the other guy's nose; there was a sucking sound we heard from across the corner, and the other guy's head deflated like a punctured beach ball and the light from the comet pulsed *on and off, on and off.* The other guy dropped straight down like a dead weight, and the guy with the big head was wiping gray stuff off his extended snout with both hands before curling it back under his chin.

Then he looked over at us.

Someone had come up behind us we hadn't heard. We jumped a foot when he yelled: *"Mierda! El Baron! El Brainiac!"*

We heard footsteps running away.

And then the baron was on us.

He grabbed Bobby by the shoulders.

If I weren't drunk I'd have been thinking faster. I remembered great-great granduncle Breck's admonition about assailants and trees. The nearest one was three blocks back and at least 50 feet tall.

I swung the rebozo-package into the baron, hard enough to shatter the piggy-bank. The baron lurched back, then got a more secure grip on Bobby.

The gold machete dropped out of the *rebozo*. I picked it up. The baron's face was closer to Bobby's, and the snout-tongue was unfolding and going toward his nose. Beyond Bobby I could see the dead guy lying crumpled on the opposite corner.

The tongue was an inch from Bobby's nose. The comet pulsed overhead.

I swung the machete and chopped off the snout-tongue as close to the baron's face as I could. The baron's tongue hit the ground, writhing like a run-over snake. The baron squealed then, a cross between a feral hog's and a giant bat's that started a ringing in my ears.

The baron ran away, gouts of blood splashing onto the street, to the south.

We ran north.

We were still running when we reached the bridge. A party of Mexican citizens was starting over the bridge toward the U.S. One of them played a guitar, and a few of them were singing.

I'd put the machete back in the rebozo with the broken bank. We ran past the singing party, and Bobby yelled to the border guards on the Mexican side: "*Adios! Gracias!*"

We ran up to the U.S. station. "Make way for a couple of Americans!" I yelled.

The U.S. guards were laughing. "Had enough of Mexico, boys?"

I stopped and turned to the party of Mexican citizens who'd followed us onto the bridge.

"How do you people *live* in that country!?" I yelled.

We ran for the truck and made for home at 100 miles an hour.

Afterword
Thin, on the Ground

Cross Plains Universe, edited by Joe Lansdale and Scott Cupp, was published for the 2006 World Fantasy Con in Austin, and the centenary of Robert E. Howard's birth.

We had a gang-signing at the convention—twenty authors, no waiting.

There were extenuating circumstances in the writing of this story. The anthology had the permission of the Howard estate, with the exception of stories about Conan, which was a separate entity.

But some jerks, who'd bought the print rights to Howard's whole output, thought this gave them permission to tell people what they could or couldn't write.

For one thing, I was told I could not use the name Breckenridge Elkins in the story. Is there any doubt in your mind who Great-Uncle Breck was? Other people's stories were affected in more major ways, and extensive rewrites ensued for them.

I was relatively unscathed, but I resented the third-party jerks' interference. Our choice: to rewrite and semi-please them, or face legal action that would hold the book up 'til after the convention, and the centenary.

Added to that, this story was very much a reaction to George W. Bush (and his benighted Republican goons). He'd had the goodwill of the world after 9/11 and had pissed it all away and had Americans acting like banana-republic secret policemen.

From the point of view of Mexico (and other Latin American neighbors), we were the ones acting like we'd lost our souls and had no lasting culture or dream life. "American Exceptionalism" indeed.

The protagonist's journey into that other, richer culture is comparable to Tim Bottoms and Jeff Bridges in McMurty's *The Last Picture Show.*

I still resent anyone telling me what I can dream about, publishing twits and George W. Bush not excepted.

Kindermarchen

Hansel was playing outside when his twin sister, Gretel, leaned out of their cottage.

"Inside!" she yelled. Her hearing was better than his. He ran into the hut.

Out their single window with the oilcloth shutters they saw the big birdlike things go by overhead. Usually they went beyond the horizon and then there were sounds and commotions far away, like distant thunder on a summer eve.

The ogres who ran their kingdom were at war with the ogres of all the other kingdoms, and had been for years. It was only lately that the battles had come nearer to their neck of the forest kingdom.

And part of it had come within their very household.

They had asked their woodcutter father why a few weeks ago.

"You want to know," he said, "why it is your stepmother, the wife of a poor man with only an axe to his name, has to go to the village every day and listen to a parade of people who plead their cases to her?"

He paused then, choosing his words. He was very tired. He had to go farther and farther each day to cut the kind of wood he needed to sell in the small village nearby. Even though it was summer, he now arrived home after dark. They did not know how he would make it through the coming winter; if indeed any of them would. Last winter there had been no food for sale in the village but dried turnips and radishes, and you could eat only so many of those.

"There is the war," he said to them that two weeks' gone morning. "Such things happen. A great edict came down from on high that children would have to be sent out of the way of the danger far to the East, to retreats. You would think that people concerned for the safety of their offspring would clamor for theirs to be the first to go. But it is not so. No one wishes to have their children leave in time of war. Who knows what may happen? Who will help with the household tasks? The harvests? All the young men were taken to help with the war long ago—and now all the young women have gone to the cities to work, or so they say. Now only the lame, the halt, old people like me, and the very young are left."

"But what does this have to do with our stepmother?" asked Hansel.

"What does *she* know?" asked Gretel.

"Children, children," said their father. "My wife, your stepmother, was appointed to the committee to decide whose children stay and whose go. This was mandated by the ogres so that it would be done impartially and by the very people affected. Hence, she has to go each day to the village and sit with the others while people come and plead for their children to be allowed to remain with them."

"But, again, why *her*?" asked Gretel.

"Dear Gretel and Hansel," their father had said that morning two weeks ago. "I know that you do not get along with your stepmother. Your poor mother died giving birth to you. I met your stepmother in my only trip to the big city far beyond our village while you were still being nursed by other women. Your stepmother was a learned woman, and when she fell in love with me, she defied her family to marry me. She lost everything: her dowry, her inheritances. It has been a hard life for her here. You must give her the credit for following her heart—no matter how disagreeable she is to you. Her intelligence was recognized by others on the committee, and she was appointed. Do you see?

"We must do all we can for the kingdom," he continued, "in these difficult times, even if that's just to keep doing the same things we've done for fifty years."

They had told him that day that they still did not understand.

"In time, you will," he had said.

This very morning he had picked up his axe, and then he had patted their heads. "I have far to go today, and then I will go to the village where your stepmother is meeting with the others, and we will be home in the evening. There is bread and cheese in the pantry. Do not let strangers into the house, and be my very good children."

So saying, he had gone.

When he and their stepmother came home that night, their father could not meet their eyes. Their stepmother went to the pegs where their clothes hung and took their few blouses and pants down and began putting them in two sacks without saying a word. She went to the pantry and put hunks of bread and cheese in each sack. Then she handed a sack to each.

"Sleep with these," she said. "You leave at dawn from the village. Your names are on the list."

"We must do *something*," whispered Gretel after her father and stepmother were asleep in their corner of the hut.

"I have a plan," said Hansel. "I will drop breadcrumbs as we go, wherever we are bound. We will get away and follow the breadcrumbs back to our village."

"Won't they come back for us when they see we are missing?" asked Gretel.

"We will worry about *that* when it happens. I don't want to leave our father, our woods, our village, even if it means having to live here with the stepmother."

"Nor I," said Gretel. "I hope your plan works, Hansel."

For an ogre, he had a kindly face. He was dressed all in black in the ogre-army fashion, but he looked like every little ogre's favorite uncle. Some ogres didn't like being around people, but he seemed to be treating it as just another of his military duties—probably better than being killed by other ogres in massed battle.

"Children," he said. "We have a long way to go to get you away from this threatened area to one of safety far behind the lines. There you will be with many many children of your own age; you will play; there are toys galore for your choosing, and you will get to eat sweets and candy to your fill."

"Can such a place exist?" asked one child to his neighbor.

"What's that?" asked the ogre-officer. "Oh, I assure you! Why, my very own children have begged me to take them there many times—I always answer the same: it's a place only for human children! You can't go there—and always they cry. I sometimes bring them home sweets from the great pile just inside the gates—I know I'm not supposed to do that, but I love my children, so I do.

"But"—he pulled himself to his fine full height—"back to duty. Though the place to which we go is wonderful—just wonderful—the way is long and hard and fraught with danger—attack from enemies, on the ground or from the air, could come at any time. We will march single file, keeping to the deep woods. We will have also to sleep in those same woods tonight; sorry, but it is two full days' march to the Children's Retreat. I will ask after you say good-bye to your parents that you not speak again to each other until we arrive at the retreat; no, not even tonight when we stop to rest—our enemies are everywhere, even in the forest in the middle of the night.

"My soldiers"—he pointed to the young ogre-soldiers who carried great packs and held the leashes of two-headed ogre-dogs. The soldiers looked bored, and the dogs lay sleepily at the soldier's feet. They carried great whips, but they were neatly coiled at their belts—"will be among you to keep order and make sure you are safe. Any orders they give you, you should treat as mine.

"You have a moment with your parents before we leave."

Hansel and Gretel said good-bye to their poor crying father. Their stepmother had not come to the village with them.

By the second hour of the march they were already tired, and by the third some of the children stumbled. Already they were beyond the limits of the farthest they had ever been from the village. Hansel noticed that the path they had taken was a new one that had not been there a month before, but already it was well-worn. He tried to dawdle toward the back of the file of children to drop the occasional crumb. After a while, he did it less and less.

They were so tired by the time the summer sun was setting that when the ogre-officer whispered to them that this was the spot where they would sleep for the night, they all slumped to the ground in their tracks.

The soldiers passed out food—a little to each child to augment what they had brought from their homes—plus some hard candy.

Then they fed the heads of their dogs alternatively. One of the dogs got in a fight with itself over a piece of meat. It made the children laugh—and be shushed—and forget about their tiredness for a moment.

"What about the bread crumbs?" asked Gretel in a whisper.

"It was a stupid idea," said Hansel.

"No talking," said a soldier far away.

The second day was worse. Some children limped from blisters or hobbled along on bruised feet. Some had lost one of their shoes, one child both, who knows where?

Through his tiredness Hansel saw that by now they were coming out of the deepest woods and were passing by streams which dashed from boulder to boulder in sprays of foam under the overhanging flank of a great mountain.

Even in this time of war, there were trees full of birds; once they saw a solitary goat high on the edge of a hillside, and hares ran from their approach, far ahead on the path.

They came out of the woods sometime after noon. Far away they saw a tall column of smoke at the edge of the horizon.

"The Childrens' Retreat!" said the officer in a low voice. "Those are the ovens where even now they bake the cakes and cookies for you! Hurry, and we shall be there in a few hours!"

Greatly heartened, they walked faster with their sore feet and tired knees and legs.

Afterword
Kindermarchen

I wrote this the morning of Friday, July 15, 2005, at Conestoga, a late-lamented convention in Tulsa, Oklahoma. I read it on Sunday afternoon and revised it the next week.

It was bounced a couple of places (Ellen Datlow; *F&SF*) before Lou Antonelli, who'd always wanted to publish something of mine, bought it for his website and paid me $25.

It was ignored by the rest of the whole world.

In the old days, I could tell exactly (within five hundred words) how long a story would be *before* I started it, by how much ground I had to cover.

I seem to have lost this ability in the last ten or so years. I imagined "Kindermarchen" to be a novelette at least ten thousand words or so and was truly surprised when I did it all in sixteen hundred words.

(Other examples—I'd imagined "Ninieslando" as a novella, and it was only sixty-two hundred words, and "The Dead Sea-Bottom

Scrolls" (coming out next year in the *Old Mars* anthology) as *way long,* which it wasn't).

I don't know why I had that ability, or why it *went away.* I'm not sure I miss it, either.

Avast, Abaft!

The *Pinafore*'s gaining on us, Your Majesty!" yelled the bosun. The Pirate King swung his spyglass aft. "Put out more sail!" he hollered. "And wet 'em down."

The ship's deck was blurred as the crew brought out canvas, lashed ropes to buckets, threw them alongsides, and hauled up seawater. Others climbed in the rigs, unfurled sails, pulled up the bucket-lines, and poured them over the filled sails.

The deck was slippery as owl snot in a matter of moments.

"Bosun. See to the cargo," said the Pirate King.

The cargo was five daughters of another general. They'd seen them on the shore having a picnic when they had stolen the ship out of Penzance. They'd put a crew out in a boat, run ashore, and grabbed them. They'd do very well for ransom, on this, the crew's first return to sea and piracy.

The pirate crew had all been Lords of the Realm who had gone bad years ago, and made a life of brigandage, but they hadn't been very good at it, being too sentimental. There'd been another in a long series of disappointments; they'd all reformed and taken their former places in society.

That hadn't worked out, either. A few weeks ago they'd had a reunion, decided to steal a ship, and take up their former ways.

"We've done well on our first day back at the job," said the Pirate King. "Well away from land; hold full of ransom. If it weren't for that damn Rackstraw and the *Pinafore*; he's closing on a course that'll suck our wind as he closes." He put down his spyglass as the ship, with more wet sail out, left the jagged dot of the *Pinafore* farther back on the horizon.

The crew, its present work done, had gathered around the Pirate King.

"What we've never heard, Your Majesty," said the bosun, "is how you yourself first became a pirate."

"Really?" asked the Pirate King. "I'm sure my story's much the same as yours. Next but one youngest son, not a chance for the peerage, waning family fortunes since the Enclosures and Industrialization—" Somewhere aboard, a mouth organ began a sprightly tune, and the Pirate King began to bob up and down.

"When I was a lad, and hardly knew a thing—

"My old pater pledged me to the service of the King.

"I powd—"

"Majesty!" yelled the bosun, the only man-jack aboard not in the circle around the Pirate King, who was looking through his spyglass. "The *Pinafore* gains again!"

"Look lively, lads! Pray for more wind. Singing continues at eight bells, attack and repel boarders notwithstanding."

After they'd wet sails and put out all canvas, the crew of the *Pinafore* had gathered around Captain Rackstraw as he told the tale of how he had first come to the Navy. A concertina played belowdecks, and Captain Rackstraw bobbed lightly. He was describing his twelve-year-old self.

"I powder-monkeyed up and I powder-monkeyed down

"And never again saw London t—"

"Captain, Captain!" yelled the first mate. "We again gain on the pirate tub!"

"Land Ho!" yelled the lookout from the crow's nest. "The pirates make for it. Two points off the starboard bow."

The concertina stopped, and the circled crew let out a sigh of disappointment.

"Sorry, lads," said Ralph Rackstraw. "When I was one of you, I know how much we all enjoyed a good sing-round. We'll have a real rip-snorter as soon as we free some captives and hang a few pirates."

"Smoke!" yelled the lookout. "Smoke from the island."

Rackstraw watched through his spyglass. The island was barely a dot, but fronds of smoke curled up from it. Then more, lighter smoke came from the left end of the place.

"Answering smoke!" shouted down the lookout. "Same four big puffs and a small one."

"That's no volcanic vent," said the Pirate King. "There are people there, and they've seen us." He turned back, looked toward the gaining *Pinafore.* "We can put the island alongships, protect our side, slug it out with the Navy ship, though we're outgunned," he said.

"Bring me the charts!" he yelled to the first mate. "We sure don't want to put in at a British provisioning station. I don't remember there being land for six hundred leagues."

"It's unknown to me, and not on the maps," said the bosun to Captain Rackstraw. "We're off the main lanes, and the Canaries and Azores are far south and behind; the Bermoothes a thousand nautical miles WSW."

The crew, including Dick Deadeye (who for some reason the rest of the crew loathed), had gathered round, hoping for some chanty or other, despite the captain's earlier words. When none was forthcoming, they dispiritedly went back to their duties.

"Ready the cannons!" said Ralph Rackstraw. "He'll put one side to shore, and run his heaviest guns out seaward, in shoaling water, so we can't cross the T on 'em. Helmsman, keep on him like he were a fox trying to go to earth, and we the lean hound."

"Aye, aye!"

The smoke continued from the two ends of the island as it grew larger.

"They're certainly talking to each other," said the bosun to the Pirate King.

"That they are, and such a small island, too. Typical high mountain in the middle. Charts show no bottom here, so it must be like one of the Pacific ones, rising straight up from the seafloor for miles. Very atypical for the Atlantic. Rest of the island probably like a ring around the mountain." He took his spyglass away from his eye. "I think I saw a waterfall off the far side, and it's inhabited, so there's fresh water. If we settle the *Pinafore,* we can at least fill our water barrels and be ready for a long run somewheres."

The ship closed with the island. "Start soundings! Helm! Make for the indentation on the port side of the island. A bay or cove, mayhaps. Look lively, make ready the cannons, O my Lords of the Realm."

"Yo!" yelled Captain Rackstraw aboard the *Pinafore*. "Make ready for battle. Break out the munitions. Riflemen, up the yards!"

Sailors ran like ants and scrambled up the ratlines. Powder monkeys disappeared belowdecks and returned with long cylinders and passed them up to the men in the rigs.

Dick Deadeye admired their precision as he lashed a wooden trough to the fore-topmast. These new munitions could scuttle any pirate tub. He nodded skyward, thanking whomever it was was responsible for science and such . . .

The stolen ship had long since disappeared around the headland. The island loomed larger, such as those he'd heard in tales from old Cook's sailors. Smoke, and the answering smoke rose up.

As the Pirate King's ship rounded on the port beam, the lookout yelled down: "There's females on the rocks."

With a squeak like a vole a half-naked girl slid off a boulder in the middle of the estuary. She slapped the water with her long green tail. Instantly, squeaks like bedsprings echoed off the island, and with a flurry of spray, like sunning turtles wakened by an otter, dozens and dozens of fish-tailed girls left their rocks and went into the lagoon. They abandoned whatever they had been doing, leaving fruit, mandolins, and half-eaten oysters atop the boulders. In an eyeflash, it was as if they had never been there.

Above on the mountain, more and more smoke rose.

"They's gone now!" came the lookout's cry.

"They's gone now?" yelled up the Pirate King. "My God, man, you went to Eton! Speak the Queen's English!"

"Your pardon, sir," shouted down the lookout. "Brevity being the soul of wit, I thought the signal more important than the noise. The females—strange indeed, sir—who formerly lay about the rocks in the estuary seem to have departed."

"See your brevity is occasionally nuanced with conjunctions and gerunds,"said his commander.

"Aye aye, sir!" yelled the lookout. "And a pleasant day to you, too, sir!"

As the *Pinafore* rounded the curve in the island, the lookout yelled there were women swimming about.

"Women?" yelled Rackstraw. "Well, we'll have to be very careful they're not in the line of fire when we close battle."

Women? the crew was thinking. The only thing they liked better than singing was the possibility of unaccompanied females on remote islands.

Here and there a long-haired head bobbed up in the water, then disappeared to reappear hundreds of yards away.

"Damn but they can swim!" said Rackstraw to the first mate.

There happened to be another pirate ship far around the island at the back edge of the lagoon, where a creek entered the river just before it dumped into the bay. The ship stood at anchor, creaking on its chain from the river current. It was wash day, and the yards hung with breeks, blouses, vests, and head-scarves.

"Damn but I'm tired," said the bosun to the first mate. "Tireder than the time in the shoals off Africa where we crawled on our hook for three days after a week of no wind."

"Why are you telling *me* this?" asked the first mate. "I was there!"

"Just passing the time while we await the captain's pleasure, which seems to be waiting," said the bosun.

"Something disturbs the fish-girls!" yelled down the lookout. "To seaward."

The captain, in his fine courtier's outfit from two centuries before, ran out of his cabin. He had been there, putting the finishing touches on his manuscript"The Great Cocodrillo of Time,"which he would post to the Secretary of the Royal Society as soon as he reached a civilized port. He hoped it would be published in the Proceedings. He had been a Fellow since before he took up his life of crime. He waved his great hook in the air. "Strike the wash! Weigh anchor! Ready the guns!"

The ship was a blur from the deck upwards. Bright clothes rained down as if from a piñata. Cannonballs rolled across the deck, men jumping and dodging.

"Move out where we have a clear field of fire!" yelled the captain. "It may be the Boy, though he usually doesn't scare the fishy-folk." He looked up toward the forested mountain."The Indians are certainly agitated," he said. Then he preened his mustaches with his glinting hook. "Perhaps for a change this will be an interesting day, methinks."

"Aye, sir," said the first mate.

As they rounded the point in the *Pinafore,* Dick Deadeye froze stock-still. It was as if he were living a dream; he was translated to a higher state of consciousness that included a perceptual breakthrough and had a paradigm shift. It was like having déjà vu two times in a row.

For he suddenly recognized this island, as if he had been there before or had been born there but had not seen it for a long time. He knew the bay, the rocks with the musical instruments and bitten-into fruit, the long curve of the lagoon, the woods on the mountain, the rising smoke.

It was as if he had heard of it long ago in a lullaby.

And then it came to him, and he went running to the ship's tailor, whose battle-station was in the repel-boarders-starboard gang.

"Pockets!" yelled Dick Deadeye. "Pockets! Run off scads of pockets. They're mad for pockets!"

"What? What?" asked the tailor's mate."What kinds of pockets? What material are the clothes? You don't just run off pockets. You put them in."

Dick Deadeye strained his brain. "Furs, I think. Skins! They have no pockets of their own."

"Who we talking about?" asked the ship's tailor, himself, putting his cutlass point-first into the *Pinafore*'s deck.

"Boys!"said Dick Deadeye."Boys bereft of parent or guardian; boys who suffered early perambulatory mishaps," he said. "I heard tell."

"Find these boys; we'll measure them, their clothes, and then see about pockets," said the ship's tailor.

"I'll pay well for pockets,"said Dick Deadeye."We'll put them as trade goods on shore, see what they take, run off more."

"Dammit, man," said the tailor's mate. "You have to put pockets *in;* what you want's bags, wallets, budgets."

"They *can't* be wanting those. I'm *sure* it's pockets they crave," said Dick Deadeye.

"See us later," said the tailor. "We've got some pirate hash to settle."

Dick Deadeye climbed back up to his battle-station in the foretopmast. Cowardly men, afraid to run off a few dozen pockets. The whole crew hated him. That was probably because they didn't like *their* day in the barrel.

—

"They're flying the Roger," yelled down the lookout to the captain. The man swung his spyglass to seaward. "Chased by a British man-o'-war."

"Prepare to sink 'em both,"said the hook-handed captain. He watched the pirate tub heave into view. "He dares to fly a Roger with a crown above it in my presence. The second because I sink all men-o'-war on sight, as you know."

"Aye, aye, Cap'n!" the crew yelled.

"Roll out Large Willy!" he yelled. The crew groaned but hopped to. It was stowed amidships, pointing forward, and took up all the room. There were two removable sections in the port and starboard gun rails to which it could be trundled. When it was run out, the breech reached halfway to the other railing and the ship listed to the mouth-side. It was the largest gun afloat. "Put him to port!" the captain yelled, pointing with his hook.

They groaned again, but with levers and movable gears swung him around.

"And for the first volley," said the captain, "give 'em a whiff o' the grape!"

They groaned louder. Why have the largest gun on any ocean if you had to come in so close as to use it for a giant blunderbuss? Why not sink the bastards with solid shot a mile off? Nevertheless they started bringing up boxes of broken horseshoes and busted anchor chains they'd bought at their last port, and shoveling them down Large Willy's barrel . . .

Before they came within sight of the river, the Pirate King said, "Drop anchor here! We make a stand to port. Run all the guns out that way. Take the two-pounders up into the rigging. Make 'em pay. Bosun—take the hostages to shore and guard 'em."

Horns blatted and whistles blew. Feet pounded. The port rail bristled with cannon and firearms.

"Just as I figured,"said Rackstraw."They're putting the island to their starboard. Very well, prepare the first volley."

Dick Deadeye, in the rigging, put his charge in the wooden trough. Good thing Buttercup had gotten them these. Anyone could have Congreve rockets as H.M.S. issue. These were the new Hale spin-stabilized kind, with angled vents for the exhaust gasses, so there was no need of the unwieldy sticks. Dick shrugged on his leather coat and face-mask with the big mica eyepieces and awaited the command from Captain Rackstraw. Five more charges waited on the arm beside him.

"On my command, volley fire,"said Rackstraw. He watched through his spyglass. "Fire!"

The air became a massed streaking of fires that converged on the pirate tub. Followed by five more volleys in rapid succession.

"Damn!" said the Pirate King. "Who the hell uses rockets except to signal anymore?" He ducked as a low one, the size of a man, crossed above the deck."We're not some heathens to be scared by noise and smoke!"

"Pardon, Your Majesty," said the first mate. "But our sails, rigging, yards, and masts are afire."

"Put out the fargin' fires!" he yelled. "Prepare to show 'em what-for."

Then there was a terrific explosion that took away all the

masts and sails and everyone on the deck of the Pirate King's ship.

"What in hell happened?" asked Rackstraw. "The whole damn thing blew up. Did they set off their own magazine?"

"Uh-oh," said the first mate. "Look, sir, beyond."

Rackstraw saw through the ghost forest of broken spars and burning canvas of the stolen ship a larger ship looming behind it, a huge cannon to port. That ship, too, flew the Roger. It was coming to get them.

On the mountainside, the smoke signals grew more frantic.

It had been a beautiful day, with only broken cloud and a bright sun, the kind made for wash day, sunning mer-folk, and Indian dances.

"Weather abaft!" shouted down the lookout to the hook-handed captain. The crew was waiting for Large Willy to cool before throwing in more powder-bags.

"Weather?" yelled up the captain. "We've not seen weather in five months. Are you drunk up there, Cecco?"

"I'm not drunk nor fooling," yelled the Italian. "And when I say weather, I mean weather!"

The captain was conflicted.

"Ahoy!" he screamed. "Simultaneously batten down the deck and prepare to fire!"

The crew looked at him.

"You heard the captain!" yelled the first mate, perplexed as the crew. "It's the caress of the hook to anyone doesn't follow orders!"

They all tried to do three things at once. It's a wonder hands or feet weren't nailed to the deck in haste.

"Weather on us!" yelled the lookout, as all their hats and scarves blew off their heads.

It was dark as midnight under Silver's skillet. They grabbed whatever they could hang on to; rails, rigging, each other. The gale whipped the lagoon to a froth. Wrack and spume obscured the man-o'-war—no telling where it was. It was useless even to yell; the words whipped away like paper.

As soon as the lookout warned of a change in the weather, Rackstraw had the ship battened down and the slow-matches taken below, and the men ordered from the riggings. It hit like the hurricane the *Pinafore* had gone through under Corcoran six years ago. The ship seemed to jump its cable length as the storm hit. "Put out a sheet anchor!" Rackstraw yelled to the crew. At least they wouldn't be dashed on the rocks, though they might be rounded.

The men tensed at the rails. All the gunports on the gun deck were opened toward where the original pirate ship had been. There was a glow through the rain, orange-yellow, where the burning ship might be.

"When the blow's over," yelled Rackstraw to the bosun, very close by, "prepare to go pick up those hostages on shore."

"If they're not blown away, too. Aye, sir," said the bosun.

Through the roiling wet, as much water as air, a shape formed, came near, from windward. After a second it turned into the second pirate ship, coming broadsides.

Everyone in both ships yelled behind their pistols, rifles, and cannon, ready to fire. It was going to be dreadful.

And then both lookouts screamed at the same instant: "JESUS H. CHRIST!" Everyone turned their heads to seaward.

A huge black galleon of two centuries gone came by, sails furled, moving against the scud and wrack, surrounded by corposantos, trailing a blur of dying sparks.

Everyone on the British man-o'-war and the huge pirate ship stood still, trying to avert their eyes (as if they could keep from looking). The ship sailed on, the storm blew off to its stern and faded away to westward. The sun came out and a gull squawked from above.

The sound of tom-toms came on the still, calm air.

"Make about to the river anchorage!" yelled the hook-handed captain.

"Prepare to pick up hostages," yelled Rackstraw.

The two ships moved apart without so much as a backward glance at each other.

Sunset. The *Pinafore* had picked up the hostages and set course back for Wales.

The hook-handed captain's ship lay at anchor off the creek and river. Out toward sea, the mermaids were back on their rocks, singing each to each.

"Yo!" yelled Jukes from the lookout. "Four specks and a spark to westward!"

"He's back!" yelled the hook-handed captain. "This time, he's mine!" He turned to the crew. "Ready Large Willy. He's still primed to fire. Maximum elevation, hit them when they cross."

The crew cranked at the elevating jacks.

The specks grew larger against the darkening east. The spark circled them like an electron in orbit, as described by Rutherford.

"Fire!" yelled the captain, bringing down his hook, and Large Willy deafened them, and a load of horseshoes and nails flew upward like shot at a grouse.

Far to the east, the *Pinafore* sailed on toward its port. Below, on the decks, Rackstraw and the officers danced with the general's daughters. Lanterns hung in the rigging and on the rails; concertinas vied with fiddles and guitars; a mouth-organ joined in. On deck, all was gaiety and merriment; the men singing along to those sentimental ballads they knew.

Far above in the rigging, Dick Deadeye leaned over the crow's nest side. He looked westward, aft, from whence they had come, and the world of the island was fading, like a half-remembered dream, on the night.

Dick Deadeye was crying.

Afterword
Avast, Abaft!

Another pre-Wheels-Coming-Off story.

Jeff VanderMeer (of Florida) was flown in for a Turkey City Writers' Workshop in September 2005.

I noticed A Lot of the workshop stories were about pirates, but just thought everyone was under the sway of Johnny Depp or something. (I remember one story where someone yelled out "Kraken storm!")

It was only after he left that I found out he and his wife Ann were publishing a pirate fantasy anthology. Then everything became clear.

I'd been thinking about this story since around 1968 when I was reading Ernest Newman's biographies of Richard Wagner. No; really.

I was trying to get The Wandering Jew into the story I'd imagined back then.

No matter what else J. M. Barrie wrote (a whole lot), he'll always be known for *Peter Pan.* Yes, sometimes it's cloying in that especially vexing Victorian-Edwardian way, and, yes, Barrie was somewhat of a Case.

But the work will live forever, like the titular creation.

Well, as soon as I started writing this (October to November, 2006) everything—Hook, Gilbert & Sullivan, especially Dick Deadeye—fell into place. (See *Topsy-Turvy* if you haven't.)

It was accepted and published in *Fast Ships, Black Sails,* published in 2008 while I was hospitalized. Hartwell picked it up for his *Year's Best Fantasy* 2009.

The title is what sailors yelled when they farted on a sailing ship.

Frogskin Cap

The sun was having one of its good days.

It came up golden and buttery, as if it were made of egg yolk.

The dawn air was light blue and clear as water. The world seemed made new and fresh, like it must have seemed in previous times.

The man in the frogskin cap (whose given name was Tybalt) watched the freshened sun as it rose. He turned to the west and took a sighting on a minor star with his astrolabe. He tickled the womb of the mother with the spider, looked away from the finger, and read off the figures to himself.

A change in light behind him gained his attention. He turned—no, not a cloud or a passing bird, something larger.

Something for which men had sometimes taken dangerous journeys of years' duration, to the farthest places of this once green and blue planet, to see and record. Now it was just a matter of looking up.

The apparent size of a big copper coin held at arm's length, a round dot was coming into, then crossing, the face of the morning sun.

He watched the planet Venus seemingly touch, then be illuminated by the light, which suffused all around it in an instant. So it was true, then: there was still an atmosphere on the planet, even so close to the sun as it had become (there was once an inner planet called Mercury, swallowed up long ago). This Venus had once been covered with dense clouds; its atmosphere now looked clear and plangent, though no doubt the sunlight beat down unmercifully on its surface.

He wished he had brought his spectacle-glass with him instead of leaving it up in his tower. But he knew of tales of others, who, looking directly into the sun with them, had become blind or sun-dazzled for years, so he sat on the wall and watched, out of the corner of his eyes, the transit of Venus 'til the big dot crossed the face of the sun and disappeared, to become another bright point of light on its far side.

He had found his frogskin cap while exploring some ruins in search of books many years ago. The skin was thin and papery, as living frogs had not been seen within the memory of the oldest living being, or his grandfather. The cap, then, was of an earlier time, when there still had been frogs to skin, probably while there still had been a Moon in the sky.

The first time he had put it on, it seemed made for him. Another sign from an earlier age to his times. From that day forward, his given name, Tybalt, was forgotten, and people only knew him as "the man in the frogskin cap."

This morning he was fishing where a stream rose full-blown from a cave in a cliff-face. He had a slim withy pole and a 6-horse-hair line. On the end of his line was a fine hook cunningly covered with feathers and fur to resemble an insect. He was angling for fish to take to town to trade to some innkeep for lodging (and a fine meal). He was bound for Joytown, where they would be celebrating the Festival of Mud, after the return of the seasonal rains, delayed by a full month this year (due no doubt to strong fluctuations in the sun).

The fish in the stream at the cave mouth were eyeless of course, which did not make them lesser eating. That they had come out of the darkness was testament to the usual dimness of light from the sun.

His artificial fly landed on the water near a rock. He twitched the line several times, setting off rings of ripples from the fly.

With a great splash, a large blind fish swallowed the fly and dove for the bottom. Tybalt used the litheness of his pole to fight the fish's run. In a moment, he had it flopping on the bank. He put it in the wet canvas fish-bag with the three others he'd already caught, and decided he had more than enough for barter.

He wrapped his line around his pole and stuck the fly into the butt of the rod. Carrying the heavy bag over his shoulder, he continued on to Joytown.

The festival was at full peak. People were in their holiday clothes, dancing to the music of many instruments, or standing swaying in place.

Those really in the spirit were in loincloths and a covering of mud, or just in mud, returned from the wet-hill slide and the mudpit below.

Tybalt was heartened to see that primitive sluice-machinery kept the slide wet. Perhaps the spirit of Rogol Domedonfors had never died through all the long centuries of Time. Not all was left to magic and sorcery in this closing down of the ages. The quest for science and knowledge still simmered below the swamps of sorcery.

"KI-YI-YI!" yelled someone at the top of the wet-hill slide, and plunging down its curving length became an ever-accelerating, ever-browner object before shooting off the end of the slide and landing with great commotion and impressive noise in the muddy pit beyond.

Polite applause drifted across the watching crowd.

Tybalt had already traded the fine mess of fish (less one for his own meal) for lodging at inn. At first, the publican, a small stout man with a gray-red beard, had said "Full-up, like all other places in this town." But as Tybalt emptied his bag on the table, the man's eyes widened. "A fine catch," he said, "and supplies being somewhat short, what with the crowd eating anything that slows a little all week . . ." He stroked his chin. "We have a maid's room; she can go home and sleep with her sisters. This mess of fish should be enough for—what?—two nights let's say. Agreed?"

They put hands together like sawing wood. "Agreed!" said Tybalt.

She was a pretty girl in less than a costume. "Kind Ladies. Strong Gentlemen," she said in a voice that carried incredibly well. "Tonight, for the first time, you will see before your very eyes the True History of the Sun!"

She stepped to one side in the cleared space before the milling crowd, now beginning to settle down. "To present this wonder to you, the greatest Mage of the age, Rogol Domedonfors, Jr."

The audacity of the *nom du stage* took Tybalt aback. The one true Rogol Domedonfors had lived ages ago, the last person dedicated to preserving science and machinery before mankind waned into its magics and superstitions.

The man anpeared in a puff of flame and billowing smoke.

"I come to you with wonders," he said, "things I learned at the green porcelain palace which is the Museum of Man."

"All wanders are known there," he continued, "though most are studied but once, then forgotten. If you but know where to look, the answers to all questions may be found."

"Behold," he said, "the sun." A warm golden glow filled the air above the makeshift stage. The glow drew down into a ball, and the simulacrum of a yellow star appeared in the wings. It moved from the east, arced overhead, and settled westward. A smaller silver ball circled around it.

"For centuries untold, the sun circled the Earth," he said. "And it had a companion called the Moon, which gave light at night after the sun had set."

Wrong, thought Tybalt, *but let's catch his drift.*

The sun-ball had dropped below the leftward stage-horizon while the Moon-ball moved slowly overhead. Then the Moon-ball swam westward while the sun began to glow and came up in dawn on the eastward of the stage.

"Oooh," said the crowd. "Ahhhh."

"'Til," said Rogol Domedonfors Jr., "Men, practicing their magick arts, conjured up a fierce dragon which ate up that Moon."

A swirling serpentine shape formed in the air between the Moon-and-Sun balls, coalescing into an ophidiaform dragon of purest black. The dragon swallowed the Moon-ball, and the sun-ball was left alone in the stage-sky.

Wrong, thought Tybalt again, *and I get your drift.*

"Not satisfied," said Rogol Domedonfors Jr., "Men, practicing their magic arts, pulled the sun closer to the Earth, even though they had to dim its light. Hence, the sun we behold today."

The sun-ball was larger and its surface redder, great prominences curled out from it, and it was freckled like the fabled Irishman of old.

"So man in his wisdom and age has given himself a sun to match his mood. Long may the Spirit of Man and his magicks last, long may that glorious sun hold sway in the sky."

There was polite applause. From far away, on the slide-hill, another moron dashed himself into the mud-pit.

It had begun to rain. They were inside the inn where Rogol Domedonfors Jr. and his companion, whose name was T'silla, lodged. T'silla placed before her a silver ball and three silvered cowbells.

"Ah!" said Tybalt. "The old game of the bells and the ball." He turned back to Rogol Domedonfors Jr.

"Great showmanship," he said. "But you know it be not true. The Moon was swallowed when Bode's inexorable law met with the unstoppable Roche's Limit!"

"True physics makes poor show," said the mage.

T'silla moved the cowbells around in a quick blur.

Tybalt pointed to the center one.

She lifted the bell to reveal the ball, quickly replaced it, moved the bells again.

Tybalt pointed to the leftward one.

She lifted that bell and frowned a little when the ball was revealed.

Listen to the rain," said Rogol Domedonfors Jr. "The crops will virtually spring up this year. There will be fairs, festivals, excitements all growing season. And then the harvest dinners."

"Aye," said Tybalt. "There was some indication that wind patterns were shifting. That the traditional seasons would be abated. Changes in the heat from the sun. Glad to see these forebodings to be proven false. Surely you ran across them when you were Curator of the Museum of Man?"

"Mostly old books," said the mage. "Not very many dealing with magick, those mostly scholarly."

"But surely . . ."

"I am certain there are many books of thought and science there," said Rogol Domedonfors Jr. "Those I leave to people of a lesser beat of mind."

T'silla let the blurred bells come to rest. She looked up at Tybalt questioningly.

"Nowhere," he said. "The ball is in your hand."

With no sign of irritation, she dropped the ball on the table and covered it with a bell, then brought the two others around.

"Then do you not return to the Museum of Man?" asked Tybalt, adjusting his frogskin cap.

"Perhaps after this harvest season is over, many months from now. Perhaps not."

T'silla moved the bells again.

From far away on the slide-hill, an idiot screamed and belly-flopped into the cloaca at its bottom.

"Give the people what they want," said Rogol Domedonfors Jr. "and they'll turn out every time."

The way southward had been arduous, though most of the country people were in an especially good, generous mood because of the signs of a bumper harvest. They invited him to sleep in their rude barns and to partake of their meager rations as if it were a feast,

It was at a golden glowing sunset after many months of travel that he came within sight of the green porcelain palace that had to be the Museum of Man.

From this distance, it looked to be intricately carved from a single block of celadon, its turrets and spires glowing softly green in the late afternoon sun. He hurried his steps while the light lasted.

A quick inspection revealed it to be everything he'd hoped for. Tome after tome in many languages; charts and maps; plans of cities long fallen to ruin. In the longer halls, exhibit after exhibit of the history of the progress of the animal and vegetal kingdoms, and of Mankind. There were machines designed for flying through the air; others seemingly made for travel beneath the seas. There were men of metal shaped like humans whose purpose he could not fathom. He had time before darkness to discover that the northenmost tower was an observatory with a fine giant spying-glass.

He found a hall of portraits of former Curators of the Museum. Just before he had parted company with Rogol Domedonfors and T'silla months ago, she had handed him a folded and sealed paper.

"What's this?" he had asked.

"There will come a time when you will need it. Open it then," she said. All these months, it had been a comforting weight in his pocket.

He travelled up the hall of portraits, pausing at the one of the original Rogol Domedonfors from long ages past. He came up the hall as if transgressing time itself, noting changes in the styles of costuming in the portraits, from the high winged collars to the off-the-shoulder straps. The last full portrait outside the curator's door was of Rogol Domedonfors Jr. Tybalt noted the faint resemblence of the features shared by he and the original—the wayward cowlick, the frown-line on one side of the mouth, the long neck. Almost impossible that the same features would skip so many generations, only to show up later in the namesake.

Last outside the door was an empty frame with four pins stuck at its center.

Tybalt reached in his pocket, took out the folded and sealed paper, broke its waxen seal, and unfolded it.

It was a drawing of himself, done in brown pencil, wearing his frogskin cap. The legend below said: "Tybalt the Scientist. 'Frogskin Cap' The last Curator of the Museum of Man." It was an excellent likeness, though the words uneased him. When had T'silla had time between the game of the bells and the ball, and early the next rainy morning when they parted, to do such a good drawing?

He pinned the drawing within the frame—it fit perfectly. It made him feel at home, as if he had a place there.

He noticed, too, that as the night had darkened, the walls of the room had begun to glow with the faintest of blue lights, which intensified as the outside grew blacker. He looked from the office-room, and the whole museum glowed likewise.

He found a writing instrument and pages of foolscap, cleared a space on the desk, and began to write on the topmost sheet:

THE TRUE AUTHENTIC HISTORY OF OUR SUN

By Tybalt, "Frogskin Cap"

Curator of the Museum of Man

He had worked through most of the night. The walls were fading as a red glow tainted eastwards.

Tybalt stretched himself. He had barefly begun outlining the main sequence of the birth, growth, senescence, and death of stars. Enough for now; there were books to consult; there was food to find. He was famished, having finished some parched corn he'd gotten at the last farmhouse before coming to the woods that led to the Museum of Man, late the afternoon before. Surely there was food somewhere hereabouts.

He went outside the green porcelain museum and turned to face the east.

The darkened sun rose lumpy as a cracked egg. Straggly whiskers of fire stood out from the chins of the sun, growing and shortening as he watched.

A curl of fire swept up out of the top of the sphere, and the surface became pocked and darkened, as if it had a disease.

The sun was having one of its bad days.

Afterword
Frogskin Cap

All the while I'm in the VA joint and not able to do much work, George R. R. Martin and Gardner Dozois are waiting for a story from me, for what is the marketing coup of the century.

Jack Vance, venerable writer and dreamer, wrote *The Dying Earth,* a novel in linked stories, on various leaky tubs he served on in WWII. It was published by the publisher of Airboy Comics (in a stab at respectability) in 1950, and was an instant classic.

Since then, he'd resisted all but one attempt (see *A Quest for Simbalis,* by Michael Shea, 1976) by others to play in his world. Since then, not again, though Vance himself set several later works in *The Dying Earth* milieu.

He'd granted Martin and Dozois the right to an original anthology set on the Dying Earth. It was the hot book to be in that year, and I'd wanted to be in it before the Unpleasantness of 2008.

Well, it was a race between my failing body and a deadline George and Gardner were holding for (over?) me.

After the hospital stay, as I said, I lived for two months with my sister Mary and her husband, Danny Hodnett, in Mississippi. About halfway thru, they went on a cruise Mary had won on an Internet sweepstakes.

I was taken down to Starkville, Mississippi, to stay with my niece Nikki and her husband (and some big woolly dogs and a dachshund) while Mary and Danny were off whooping it up and shooting skeet off the port bow, etc.

I'd tried to start *The Dying Earth* story while in the hospital, buying a batch of legal pads and some fairly pen-like felt-tip markers. I got around 100 words a page in writing I could see and gave it up as a bad idea around September 30th.

Back to Starkville, November 2008. I sit down at a desk in Nikki's house and wrote the sumbitch in three days, the first writing I'd done in six months. George and Gardner bought it, of course.

I'd had someone bring my copy of *The Dying Earth* up to the VA hospital earlier, and read it with a big magnifying glass, for the second time since 1962.

I'd read it in the same Lancer SF Classics paperback edition then, sitting at the time under a magnolia tree, between ninth grade and sophomore year of high school.

The book I reread in 2008 was a different book than in 1962 (I like to think I had matured in the intervening years). But I think *The Dying Earth* had become a better, denser work with the passage of half a century or so.

The one element I couldn't find was the "frogskin cap" that gave me my title, which had stuck in my mind since the 1962 reading. I added some stuff Vance couldn't have known about in 1950

nd, had been to accompany the officer to the listening
le the plaster dead horse, thirty feet in front of their
e. That the l.p. was tapped into the German field tele-
tem (as they were into the British) meant that some poor
l had to crawl the quarter-mile through No Man's Land
k, find a wire, and tap into it. (Sometimes after doing so,
l they'd tied into a dead or abandoned wire.) Then he'd
efully crawl back to his own line, burying the wire as he
nd making no noise, lest he get a flare fired off for his

vas usually done when wiring parties were out on both
ng noises of their own, so routine that they didn't draw
n or small-arms fire.

had evidently been lots of unidentified talk on the
to hear the rumours. The officers were pretty close-
u didn't admit voices were there in a language you
rstand and could make no report on). Officers from
l Staff had been to the l.p. in the last few nights and
with nothing useful. A few hours in the mud and the
robably done them a world of good, a break from
r routines in the chateau that was HQ miles back of

ttle information that reached the ranks was, as the cap-
robably Hungarian, or some other Balkan sub-tongue."
the case, and was sending in some language experts
they said.

looked through the slit just below the neck of the fake
, nothing. He cradled his rifle next to his chest. This
een almost as cold as any January he remembered. At
w had not come yet, turning everything to cold wet
.

(and before)—the extinction of many frog species, etc., and tied them in with the far future of a senescent Earth Vance had pictured.

I also tied him in with H. G. Wells' vision of the far future from *The Time Machine* ("the green porcelain palace"—why not have it be the Museum of Man?).

I was proud of the story, and pleased that I could still write AT ALL.

Ninies

The captain had a puzzled look
the right earphone and frowned
"Lots of extraneous chatter
some Fritz's have been replaced
to be in some language I don't s
Tommy peered out into the
And of course could see nothin
a bloated dead horse that had la
week ago the plaster replica had
the camouflage shops far behin
party had had to get out in the
thing with the plaster one, but
and burst months before.
They had come back nas
had been sent back to the bath
luxury of a hot bath and a cle
Tommy at the time.
Tommy's sentry duty th
ing into the blackness over th

Man's La
post insi
trench lin
phone sys
sapper ha
in the dar
they'd fin
had to ca
retreated,
trouble.
This
sides, mak
illuminati
There
lines lately
lipped (yo
didn't und
the Genera
came back
dark had
their regul
the line.
What l
tain said, "
HQ was o
soon. Or so
Tommy
horse. Agai
March had
least the th
clinging mu

There was the noise of slow dragging behind them, and Tommy brought his rifle up.

"Password" said the captain to the darkness behind the horse replica.

"Ah—St. Agnes Eve . . . ," came a hiss.

"Bitter chill it was," said the captain. "Pass."

A lieutenant and a corporal came into the open side of the horse. "Your relief, sir," said the lieutenant.

"I don't envy you your watch," said the captain. "Unless you were raised in Buda-Pesh."

"The unrecognizable chatter again?" asked the junior officer.

"The same."

"Well, I hope someone from HQ has a go at it soon," said the lieutenant.

"Hopefully."

"Well, I'll give it a go," said the lieutenant. "Have a good night's sleep, sir."

"'Very well. Better luck with it than I've had." He turned to Tommy. "Let's go, Private."

"Sir!" said Tommy.

They crawled the thirty feet or so back to the front trench on an oblique angle, making the distance much longer, and they were under the outermost concertina wire before they were challenged by the sentries.

Tommy went immediately to his funk hole dug into the wall of the sandbagged parapet. There was a nodding man on look-out; others slept in exhausted attitudes as if they were, like the l.p. horse, made of plaster.

He wrapped his frozen blanket around himself and was in a troubled sleep within seconds.

———

"Up for morning stand-to!" yelled the sergeant, kicking the bottom of his left boot.

Tommy came awake instantly, the way you do after a few weeks at the Front.

It was morning stand-to, the most unnecessary drill in the army. The thinking behind it was that, at dawn, the sun would be full in the eyes of the soldiers in the British and French trenches, and the Hun could take advantage of it and advance through No Man's Land and surprise them while they were sun-dazzled. (The same way that the Germans had *evening* stand-to in case the British made a surprise attack on them out of the setting sun.) Since no attacks were ever made across the churned and wired and mined earth of No-Man's Land by either side unless preceded by an artillery barrage of a horrendous nature, lasting from a couple, to in one case, twenty-four hours, of constantly falling shells, from the guns of the other side, morning stand-to was a sham perpetrated by long-forgotten need from the early days of this Great War.

The other reason it was unnecessary was that this section of the Line that ran from the English Channel to the Swiss border was on a salient, and so the British faced more northward from true east, so the sun, instead of being their eyes, was a dull glare off the underbrims of their helmets somewhere off to their right. The Hun, if he ever came across the open, would be sidelit and would make excellent targets for them.

But morning stand-to had long been upheld by tradition and the lack of hard thinking when the Great War had gone from one of movement and tactics in the opening days to the one of attrition and stalemate it had become since.

This part of the front had moved less than one hundred yards, one way or the other, since 1915.

Tommy's older brother, Fred, had died the year before on the first day of the Somme Offensive, the last time there had been any real movement for years. And that had been more than fifty miles up the Front.

Tommy stood on the firing step of the parapet and pointed his rifle at nothing in particular to his front through the firing slit in the sandbags. All up and down the line, others did the same.

Occasionally some Hun would take the opportunity to snipe away at them. The German sandbags were an odd mixture of all types of colors and patterns piled haphazardly all along their parapets. From far away, they formed a broken pattern, and the dark and light shades hid any break, such as a firing slit, from easy discernment. But the British sandbags were uniform, and the firing and observation slits stood out like sore thumbs, something the men were always pointing out to their officers.

As if on cue, there was the sound of smashing glass down the trench and the whine of a ricocheting bullet. A lieutenant threw down the trench periscope as if it were an adder that had bitten him.

"Damn and blast!" he said aloud. Then to his batman "Requisition another periscope from regimental supply." The smashed periscope lay against the trench wall, its top and the mirror inside shot clean away by some sharp-eyed Hun. The batman left, going off in defile down the diagonal communication trench that led back to the reserve trench.

"Could have been worse," someone down the trench said quietly. "Could have been his head." There was a chorus of wheezes and snickers.

Humour was where you found it, weak as it was.

Usually both sides were polite to each other during their respective stand-tos. And afterwards, at breakfast and the evening meal. It wasn't considered polite to drop a shell on a man who'd just taken a forkful of beans into his mouth. The poor fellow might choke.

Daytime was when you got any rest you were going to get. Of course there might be resupply, or ammunition, or food-toting details, but those came up rarely, and the sergeants were good about remembering who'd gone on the last one, and so didn't send you too often.

There was mail call, when it came, then the midday meal (when and if it came) and the occasional equipment inspection. Mostly you slept unless something woke you up.

Once a month, your unit was rotated back to the second trench, where you mostly slept as well as you could, and every third week to the reserve trench, far back, in which you could do something besides soldier. Your uniform would be cleaned and deloused, and so would you.

In the reserve trench was the only time your mind could get away from the War and its routine. You could get in some serious reading, instead of the catch-as-catch kind of the first and second trenches. You could get a drink and eat something besides bully beef and hardtack if you could find anybody selling food and drink. You could see a moving picture in one of the rear areas, though that was a long hike, or perhaps a music-hall show, put on by one of the units, with lots of drag humour and raucous laughter at not very subtle material. (Tommy was sure the life of a German soldier was much the same as his.)

It was one of the ironies of these times that in that far-off golden summer of 1914, when "some damn fool thing in the Balkans" was leading to its inevitable climax, Tommy's brother, Fred, who was then eighteen, had been chosen as a delegate of the Birmingham Working-Men's Esperanto Association to go as a representative to the 24th Annual Esperanto Conference in Basel, Switzerland. The Esperanto Conference had been to take place in the last days of July and the first days of August. (Fred had been to France before with a gang of school chums and was no stranger to travel.)

The Esperanto Conference was to celebrate the 24th anniversary of Zamenhof's artificial language, invented to bring better understanding between peoples through the use of an easy-to-learn, totally regular invented language—the thinking being that if all people spoke the same language (recognizing a pre-Babel dream), they would see that they were all one people, with common dreams and goals, and would slowly lose nationalism and religious partisanship through the use of the common tongue.

There had been other artificial languages since—Volapuk had had quite a few adherents around the turn of the century—but none had had the cachet of Esperanto: the first and best of them.

Tommy and Fred had been fascinated by the language for years (Fred could both speak and write it with an ease that Tommy had envied).

What had surprised Fred, on arriving in Switzerland three years before, was that these representatives of this international conference devoted to better understanding among peoples were as acrimonious about their nations as any bumpkin from a third-rate country run by a tin-pot superstitious chieftain. Almost from the first, war and the talk of war divided the true believers from the lip-service toadies. The days were rife with desertions, as first one country then another announced mobilizations. By foot, by horse, by motor-car and train, and, in one case, aeroplane, the delegates left the conference, to join up in the coming glorious adventure of war that they imagined would be a quick, nasty, splendid little one, over "before the snow flew."

By the end of the conference, only a few delegates were left, and they had to make hurried plans to return home before the first shots were fired.

His brother, Fred, now dead, on the Somme, had returned to England on August 2, 1914, just in time to see a war no one wanted (but all had hoped for) declared. He, like so many idealists of all classes and nations, had joined up immediately.

Now Tommy, who had been three years younger at the time, was all that was left to his father and mother. He had of course been called up in due time, just before news of his brother's death had reached him.

And now here he was, in a trench of frozen mud, many miles from home, with night falling, when the sergeant walked by and said, "Fall out for wiring detail."

Going on a wiring party was about the only time you could be in No Man's Land with any notion of safety. As you were repairing and thickening your tangle of steel, so were the Germans doing the same to theirs a quarter-mile away.

Concertina wire, so haphazard-appearing from afar, was not there to stop an enemy assault, though it slowed that, too. The wire was there to funnel an enemy into narrower and tighter channels, so the enemy's course of action would become more and more constricted—and where the assault would finally slow against the impenetrable lanes of barbed steel was where your defensive machine-gun fire was aimed. Men waiting to go over, under, through, or around the massed wire were cut to ribbons by .303 caliber bullets fired at the rate of five hundred per minute.

Men could not live in such iron weather.

So you kept the wire repaired. At night. In the darkness, the sound of unrolling wire and muffled mauls filled the space between the lines. Quietly cursing men hauled the rolls of barbed wire over the parapets and pushed and pulled them out to where some earlier barrage (which was always supposed to cut all the wire but never did) had snapped some strands or blown away one of the new-type posts (which didn't have to be hammered in but were screwed into the ground as if the earth itself were one giant champagne cork).

Men carried wire, posts, sledges in the dark, out to the place where the sergeant stood.

"Two new posts here," he said, pointing at some deeper blackness. Tommy could see nothing, anywhere. He put his coil of wire on the ground, immediately gouging himself on the barbs of an unseen strand at shoulder height. He reached out—felt the wire going left and right.

"Keep it quiet," said the sergeant. "Don't want to get a flare up our arses." Illumination was the true enemy of night work.

Sounds of hammering and work came from the German line. Tommy doubted that anyone would fire off a flare while their own men were out in the open.

He got into the work. Another soldier screwed in a post a few feet away.

"Wire," said the sergeant. "All decorative-like, as if you're trimming the Yule tree for Father Christmas. We want Hans and Fritz to admire our work, just before they cut themselves in twain on it."

Tommy and a few others uncoiled and draped the wire, running it back and forth between the two new posts and crimping it in with the existing strands.

Usually you went out, did the wiring work, and returned to the trench, knowing you'd done your part in the War. Many people had been lost in those times: there were stories of disoriented men making their way in the darkness, not to their own but to the enemy's trenches, and being killed or spending the rest of the war as a P.O.W.

Sometimes Tommy viewed wiring parties as a break in the routine of stultifying heat, spring and fall rains, and mud, bone-breaking winter freezes. It was the one time you could stand up in relative comfort and safety, and not be walking bent over in a ditch.

There was a sudden rising comet in the night. Someone on Fritz's side had sent up a flare. Everybody froze—the idea was not to move at all when No Man's Land was lit up like bright summer daylight. Tommy, unmoving, was surprised to see Germans caught out in the open, still also as statues, in front of their trench, poised in attitudes of labor on their wire.

Then who had fired off the flare?

It was a parachute flare and slowly drifted down while it burned the night to steel-furnace-like brilliance. There were pops and cracks and whines from both trenchlines as snipers on each side took advantage of the surprise bounty of lighted men out in the open.

Dirt jumped up at Tommy's feet. He resisted the urge to dive for cover, the nearest being a shell crater 20 feet away. Any movement would draw fire, if not to him, to the other men around him. They all stood stock-still; he saw droplets of sweat on his sergeant's face.

From the German line a trench mortar coughed.

The earth went upwards in frozen dirt and a shower of body parts.

———

He felt as if he had been kicked in the back.

His right arm was under him. His rifle was gone. The night was coming back in the waning flickering light from the dying flare. He saw as he lay his sergeant and a couple of men crawling away toward their line. He made to follow them. His legs wouldn't work.

He tried pushing himself up with his free arm; he only rolled over on the frozen earth. He felt something warm on his back quickly going cold.

No, he thought, I can't die like this out in No Man's Land. He had heard, in months past, the weaker and weaker cries of slowly dying men who'd been caught out here. He couldn't think of dying that way.

He lay for a long time, too tired and hurt to try to move. Gradually his hearing came back; there had only been a loud whine in his ears after the mortar shell had exploded.

He made out low talk from his own trench, twenty or so yards away. He could imagine the discussion now. Should we go out and try to get the wounded or dead? Does Fritz have the place zeroed in? Where's Tommy? He must have bought a packet.

Surprisingly, he could also hear sounds which must be from the German line—quiet footsteps, the stealthy movement from shell-hole to crater across No Man's Land. The Germans must have sent out searching parties. How long had he lain here? Had there been return fire into the German work parties caught in the open by the flare? Were the British searching for their own wounded? Footsteps came nearer to him. Why weren't the sentries in his own trench challenging them? Or firing? Were they afraid that it was their own men making their ways back?

The footsteps stopped a few yards away. Tommy's eyes had adjusted to the darkness after the explosion. He saw vague dark shapes all around him. Through them moved a lighter man-shape. It moved with quick efficiency, pausing to turn over what Tommy saw now was a body near him.

It was at that moment that another weaker flare bloomed in the sky from the German trench, a red signal flare of some kind. In its light, Tommy saw the figure near him continue to rifle the body that lay there.

Tommy saw that the figure was a Chinaman. What was a Chinaman doing here in No Man' s Land?

Perhaps, Tommy thought, coughing, he speaks English. Maybe I can talk to him in Esperanto? That's what the language was invented for.

He said, in Esperanto, the first sentence he had ever learned in the language.

—Could you direct me to the house of the family Lodge?

The Chinaman stopped. His face broke into a quizzical look in the light of the falling flare. Then he smiled, reached down to his belt, and brought up a club. He came over and hit Tommy on the head with it.

He woke in a clean bed, in clean sheets, in clean underwear, with a hurt shoulder and a headache. He was under the glare of electric lights, somewhere in a clean and spacious corridor.

He assumed he was far back of the Lines in a regimental hospital. How he had gotten here he did not know.

A man came to the foot of the bed. He wore a stethoscope.

—Ah,—he said.—You have awakened.—He was speaking Esperanto.

"Am I in the division hospital?" asked Tommy in English.

The man looked at him uncomprehendingly.

He asked the same again, in Esperanto, searching for the words as he went.

—Far from it.—said the man.—You are in our hospital, where you needn't ever worry about the war you have known again. All will be explained later.

—Have I been taken to Switzerland in my sleep?—asked Tommy. —Am I in some other neutral country?

—Oh , you're in some neutral country all right. But you're only a few feet from where you were found. And I take it you were under the impression it was a Chinese who rescued you. He's no Chinese—he would be offended to be called such—but Annamese, from French Indo-China. He was brought over here in one of the first levees early in the War. Many of them died that first winter, a fact the survivors never forgot. How is it you speak our language?

—I was in the Esperanto Union from childhood on. I and my brother, who's now dead. He both wrote and spoke it much better than I.

—It was bound to happen—said the man.—You can imagine Ngyen's surprise when you spoke so, dressed in a British uniform. When you spoke, you marked yourself as one of us; he thought to bring you back the most expedient way possible, which was unconscious.

—The doctor tended your wounds—very nasty ones from which you probably would have perished had not you been brought here..

—Where is here?—asked Tommy.

—Here—said the man—is a few feet below No Man's Land—I'm sure the ex-captain will explain it all to you. It's been a while since someone in your circumstances joined us. Most of us came in the early days of the war, as soon as the lines were drawn, or were found, half-mad or wounded between the lines, and had to be brought back to health and sanity. You appear to us, wounded all the same, but already speaking the language. You'll fit right in.

—Are you British? French? German?—asked Tommy.

The man laughed. —Here—he said—none of us are of any nationality any longer. Here, we are all Men.

He left. Eventually, the doctor came in and changed the dressing on his shoulder and gave him a pill.

The ex-captain came to see him. He was a small man, dressed in a faded uniform, with darker fabric at the collar in the shape of captain's bars.

—Welcome to Ninieslando—he said.

—It's very clean—said Tommy—I'm not used to *that*.

—It's the least we can do—he said, sweeping his hand around, indicating All That Out There.

—You'll learn your way around—he continued.—You have the great advantage of already speaking our language, so you won't have to be going to classes. We'll have you on light duties till your wounds heal.

—I'm very rusty—Tommy said.—I'm out of practice. My brother was the scholar, he spoke it 'til the day he was killed on the Somme.

—We could certainly have used him here—said the ex-captain.

—Where we are—he continued, going into lecture-mode—is several feet below No Man's Land. We came here slowly, one by one, in the course of the War. The lost, the wounded, the abandoned, and, unfortunately, the slightly mad. We have dug our rooms and tunnels, tapped into the combatant's field-phones and electrical lines, diverted their water to our own uses. Here we are building a society of Men to take over the Earth after this War finally ends. Right now our goal is to survive the War—to do that we have to live off their food, water, lights, their clothing and equipment, captured at night on scavenging parties. We go into their trench lines and take what we need. We have better uses for it than killing other men.

—There are 5,600 of us in this sector. Along the whole four hundred mile Western Front, there are half a million of us, waiting our time to come out and start the New World of brotherhood. We are the first examples of it; former combatants living in harmony with a common language and common goals, undeterred by the War itself, a viable alternative to nationalism and bigotry. You can imagine the day when we walk out of here.

Tommy held out his hand. The ex-captain shook it. —It's good to finally meet a real idealist—said Tommy.—So many aren't.

—You'll see—said the ex-captain.—There's much work to be done while we wait, and it's easy to lose sight of the larger goals while you're scrounging for a can of beans. The War has provided for us, only to the wrong people. People still combatants, who still believe in the War.

—For make no mistake—he said—The Hun is not the enemy. The British are not the enemy. Neither your former officers nor the General Staff are the enemy. The *War* is the enemy. It runs itself on the fears of the combatants. It is a machine into which men are put and turned into memories.

—Every illness, self-inflicted wound, or accident is referred to by both sides as "wastage"—*perdajo*—meaning that the death did not contribute in any way to a single enemy soldier's death.

—A man being in the War, to War's way of thinking, was wasted. The idea has taken over planning. The War is thinking for the General Staff. They have not had a single idea that was not the War's in these three years.

—So we take advantage. A flare fired off in the night when no one expects it brings the same result as if we had a regimental battery of Krupp howitzers. The War provides the howitzers to us as well as to the combatants.

—I need not tell you this—he said. —I'm going on like Wells's wandering artilleryman in *War of the Worlds.* Everyone here has to quit thinking like a combatant and begin to think like a citizen of Ninieslando. What can we do to take War out of the driver's seat? How do we plan for the better world while War is making that world cut its own throat? We are put here to bring some sense to it: to stay War's hand. Once mankind knows that War is the enemy, he will be able to join us in that bright future. Zamenhof was right: Esperanto will lead the way!

—Good luck—he said, making ready to leave,—new citizen of Ninieslando.

Their job today, some weeks after the ex-captain's visit, was to go to a French supply point, load up, and bring rations back by secret ways to Ninieslando, where their cooks would turn it into something much more palatable than the French ever thought of making. They had on parts of French uniforms; nobody paid much attention this late in the day and the War, if the colors were right. Tommy had a French helmet tied by its chin strap to his belt in the manner of a jaunty French workingman.

They took their place in a long line of soldiers waiting. They moved up minute by minute 'til it was their turn to be loaded up.

"No turnips," said the sergeant with them, who had been at Verdun.

"Ah, but of course," said the supply sergeant. "As you request." He made an impolite gesture.

They took their crates and sacks and followed the staggering line of burdened men returning to the trenches before them. The connecting trench started as a path at ground level and slowly sank as the walls of the ditch rose up around them as they stepped onto the duckboards. Ahead of them the clump-clump-clump of many feet echoed. The same sounds rose behind them.

Somewhere in the diagonal trench between the second and front line, they simply disappeared with the food at a blind turn in the connecting trench.

They delivered the food to the brightly lit electric kitchens below the front line.

—Ah, good—said a cook, looking into a sack,—Turnips!

He waited at a listening post with an ex-German lieutenant.

—Lots a chatter tonight—he said to Tommy.—They won't notice much when we talk with other sectors later.

—Of course—said Tommy.—The combatants are tapped into each other's lines, trying to get information. They hear not only their enemies, but us.

—And what do they do about it?—asked the ex German.

—They try to figure out what language is being spoken. Our side was puzzled.

—They usually think it some Balkan tongue.—said the ex-German.—Our side thought it could be Welsh or Basque. Did you ever hear it?

—No, only officers listened.

—You would have recognized it immediately. But war has taught the officers that enlisted men are lazy illiterate swine, only interested in avoiding work and getting drunk. What language knowledge could they have? Otherwise, they would be officers. Is it not true?

—Very true.—said Tommy.

A week later, Tommy was in the brightly lit library, looking over the esoteric selection of reading matter filched from each side. Field manuals, cheap novels, anthologies of poetry, plays in a dozen languages. There were some books in Esperanto, most published before the turn of the century. Esperanto had had a great vogue then, before the nations determined it was all a dream and went back to their armaments races and their "places in the sun." There were, of course, a few novels translated into Esperanto.

There was also the most complete set of topographical maps of the Front imaginable. He looked up this sector; saw the plan of Ninieslando's tunnels and corridors, saw that even the British listening post had the designation "fake plaster horse." He could follow the routes of Ninieslando from the Swiss border to the English Channel (except in those places where the front-line trenches were only yards apart; there was hardly room for excavation there without calling the attention of both sides to your presence). Here, Ninieslando was down to a single tunnel no wider than a communications trench up on the surface to allow exchanges between sectors.

Either side up above would give a thousand men in return for any map of the set.

That meant that the work of Ninieslando went on day and night, listening and mapping out the smallest changes in the topography. The map atop each pile in the drawer was the latest, dated most recently. You could go through the pile and watch the War backwards to—in some cases—late 1914, when the Germans had determined where the Front would be by pulling back to the higher ground, even if only a foot or two more in elevation. Ninieslando had been founded then, as the War became a stalemate.

In most cases, the lines had not changed since then, except to become more churned up, muddier, nastier. Occasionally, they would shift a few feet, or a hundred yards, due to some small advance by one side or the other. Meanwhile, Ninieslando became more complex and healthier as more and more men joined.

As the ex-captain had said:—The War made us the best engineers, machinists, and soldiers ever known. A shame to waste all that training. So we used it to build a better world, underground.

Tommy looked around the bright shiny library. He could spend his life here, building a better world indeed.

For three nights, each side had sent out raiding parties to the other's line. There had been fierce fighting as men all through the sector stomped or clubbed each other to death.

It had been a bonanza for Ninieslando's scavenging teams. They had looted bodies and the wounded of everything usable: books, food, equipment, clothing. They had done their work efficiently and thoroughly, leaving naked bodies all through No Man's Land. The moans of the dying followed them as they made their way back down through the hidden entrances to Ninieslando.

Tommy, whose shoulder wound had healed nicely, lay in his clean bunk after dropping off his spoils from the scavenging at the sector depot. The pile of goods had grown higher than ever—more for Ninieslando. He had a copy of *The Oxford Book of English Verse* open on his chest. The language was becoming lost to him, he had not spoken it in so long. He was now thinking, and even dreaming, in Esperanto. As well it should be. National languages were a drag and a stumbling block to the human race. He read a few poems, then closed the book. For another day, he thought, when we look back with a sort of nostalgia on a time when national languages kept men separated. He imagined the pastoral poems of the future, written in Esperanto, with shepherds and nymphs recalling lines of English each to each, as if it were a lost tongue like Greek or Latin. He yearned for a world where such things could be.

The field phones had been strangely silent for a day or so. But it was noticed that couriers went backwards and forwards from trench to observation post to headquarters. On both sides. Obviously, something was up. A courier was waylaid in the daylight, a dangerous undertaking, but there were no paper orders on him. The kidnapping team drew the line at torture, so reported that the orders must be verbal. Perhaps, by coincidence, both sides were planning assaults at the same time to break the stalemate. It would be a conflagration devoutly to be desired by Ninieslando.

Of course, the War had made it so both sides would lose the element of surprise when the batteries of both sides opened in barrages at the same time, or nearly so. Ninieslando waited—whatever happened, No Man's Land would be littered with the dead and dying, ripe for the picking.

—Too quiet—said someone in the corridor.

—They've never gone this long off the telephones—said another.

Tommy walked the clean corridor. He marveled that only a few feet overhead was a world of *ekskremento* and *malpurajo* fought over by men for three years. Here was a shinier, cleaner world than anything man had achieved on the surface.

It was just about then that the first shells of the expected barrage began to fall above his head. Dust drifted down from the ceiling. Parts of the wall buckled and shook.

Tommy realized that he was under the middle of No Man's Land. Unless their aim was very bad indeed, the artillerymen of neither side should be making their shells land here. They should be aiming for the front trench of the other side.

Ninieslando shook and reeled from the barrage. The lights went out as shells cut a line somewhere.

Tommy struck a match, found the electric torch in its niche at the corridor crossing. He turned it on and made his way to the library.

Then it got ominously quiet. The barrage ceased after a very short while. Who was firing a five-minute barrage in the wrong place? Had they all gone crazy up there?

He entered the library, shined his torch around. A few books had fallen from the shelves; mostly it was untouched.

He sat at a table. There was some noise in the corridor at the far end. A bloodied man ran in, his eyes wild, screaming.—*Tri rugo bendos!*—Three red bands!—Was he speaking metaphorically? Three Marxist gangs? Or like Sherlock Holmes, literally, as in "The Speckled Band"? What did he mean? Tommy went to grab him, but he was gone, out of the library, still yelling.

Tommy went down the hall and up a series of steps to an observation post with two viewing slits, one looking northeast, the other southwest.

What he saw looking northeast was astounding. In broad daylight, German soldiers, rifles up, bayonets fixed, were advancing. They probed the ground and debris as they came on. On the left sleeve of every soldier were three red stripes on a white background.

Tommy turned to the other slit, wondering why there was no rifle or machine-gun fire mowing down the line of Germans.

What he saw made his blood freeze. From the other direction, British and French soldiers also advanced in the open. On their right arms were pinned three red stripes on a white background. As he watched, several soldiers disappeared down an embankment. There was the sound of firing. A Ninieslandoja, with no stripes on his sleeve, staggered out and died in the dirt. The firing continued, getting fainter.

The sound of firing began again, far off down the corridor below.

Tommy took off for the infirmary.

There were many kinds of paint down at the carpentry shop, but very little approached red, the last color you'd want on a battlefield.

When Tommy ran into the infirmary, he found the ex-captain there before him. The man was tearing bandages into foot-long pieces.

Tommy went to the medicine chest and forced his way into it. Bottles flew and broke.

—They've finally done it!—said the ex-captain.—They've gotten together just long enough to get rid of us. Our scavenging last week must have finally pushed them over into reason.

Tommy took a foot-long section of bandages and quickly painted three red stripes on it with the dauber on a bottle of mercurochrome. He took one, gave it to the ex-captain, did one for himself.

—First they'll do for us—he said.—Next, they'll be back to killing each other. This is going on up and down the whole Western Front. I never thought they could keep such a plan quiet for so long.

The ex-captain headed him a British helmet and a New Model Army web-belt.—Got your rifle? Good, try to blend in. Speak English. Good luck.—He was gone out the door.

Tommy took off the opposite way. He ran toward where he thought the Germans might be.

The sound of firing grew louder. He realized he might now be a target for Ninieslanders, too. He stepped around a corridor junction and directly in front of a German soldier. The man raised his rifle barrel towards the ceiling.

"Anglander?" the German asked

—j— "Yes," said Tommy. lifting his rifle also.

"More just behind me," Tommy added. "Very few of the undergrounders in our way." The German looked at him in incomprehension. He looked farther back down the corridor Tommy had come from.

There was the noise of more Germans coming up the other hall. They lifted their rifles, saw his red stripes, lowered them.

Tommy moved with them as they advanced farther down the corridors, marveling at the construction. There was some excitement as a Ninieslander bolted from a room down the hallway and was killed in a volley from the Germans.

"Good shooting," said Tommy.

Eventually, they heard the sound of English.

"My people," said Tommy. He waved to the Germans and walked toward the voices.

A British captain with drawn pistol stood in front of a group of soldiers. The bodies of two Ninieslanders lay on the floor beside them.

—And what rat have we forced from his hole?—asked the captain in Esperanto.

Tommy kept his eyes blank.

"Is that Hungarian you're speaking, sir?" he asked, the words strange on his tongue.

"Your unit?" asked the captain.

"1st King's Own Rifles," said Tommy. "I was separated and with some Germans."

"Much action?"

"A little, most of the corridors are empty. They're off somewheres, sir."

"Fall in with my men 'til we can get you back to your company, when this is over. What kind of stripes you call those? Is that iodine?"

"Mercurochrome, I believe," said Tommy. "Supply ran out of the issue. Our stretcher-bearers used field expedients." He had a hard time searching for the right words.

Esperanto phrases kept leaping to mind. He would have to be careful, especially around this officer.

They searched out a few more rooms and hallways, found nothing. From far away, whistles blew.

"That's recall," said the captain. "Let's go."

Other deeper whistles sounded from far away, where the Germans were. It must be over.

They followed the officer 'til they came to boardings that led outside to No Man's Land.

The captain left for a hurried consultation with a group of field-grade officers. He returned in a few minutes.

"More work to do," he said. A detail brought cans of petrol and set them down nearby.

"We're to burn the first two corridors down. You, you, you," he said, indicating Tommy last. "Take these cans, spread the petrol around. The signal is three whistle blasts. Get out as soon as you light it off. Everyone got matches? Good."

They went back inside, the can heavy in Tommy's hands. He went up to the corridor turning, began to empty petrol on the duckboard floor.

He saved a little in the bottom of the can. He idly sloshed it around and around.

Time enough to build the better world tomorrow. Many, like him, must have made it out, to rejoin their side or get clean away in this chaos.

After this War is over, we'll get together, find each other, start building that new humanity on the ashes of this old world.

The three whistles came. Tommy struck a match, threw it onto the duckboard flooring, and watched the petrol catch with a *whooshing* sound.

He threw the can after it, and walked out into the bright day of the new world waiting to be born.

Afterword
Ninieslando

This was, up until last year, the major work I did after the hospitalization.

Once again, for George and Gardner's *Warriors,* an anthology of warriors throughout all times and places.

I'd done research for this before May 2008 (and forgot most of it by the time I wrote this).

Fresh from the triumph of finishing ANYTHING for *Songs of the Dying Earth,* and finally back in Austin, I sat at Martha Grenon's kitchen table in January of 2009 and wrote "Ninieslando" and sent it off to Gardner ("the muscle of the operation"). Once again, they'd been holding the anthology (not for me, this time, but for some mainstream high-tone hotshots).

I'd first come across the central idea in Paul Fussell's *The Great War and Modern Memory.* (His book first appeared in 1975 and has been in print since. It's the only book you'll ever need to read about

WWI, because it isn't about the war, per se, but about all the cultural baggage the combatants brought to it.)

The central idea of the story is in his chapter "Myth, Ritual and Romance"—that there was a lost group of men (from both sides) living in No Man's Land off the equipment, food, and bodies of the dead and wounded—like super ghouls. Where the enemy was no longer the enemy, but the War.

Well, I tried to imagine that, and added my own (not so far-fetched) idea—that they would be speaking Esperanto.

Esperanto was an artificial invented language, perfectly regular once you knew the rules, made by a guy named Zamenhof in the late 1890s. It (and Volapük) had quite a fad and following in the nineties and early Edwardian Age. It was promoted as a unifying language (if people all spoke the same, how could they fight and have national differences? The story about the delegates all leaving the International Esperanto Conference to run home and join up in August 1914 is *true*).

As late as the 1950s, I'm told, Forrest J. Ackerman and the actor Leo G. Carroll talked the night away in Esperanto—they'd learned as children—when Carroll saw Ackerman's Esperanto bumper sticker on the car parked outside.

Once I had the situation and the language, I was on my way, trying to imagine what life would be like in the Ninieslando.

When this was published, somebody criticized my Esperanto, which I'd mostly forgotten by the time I wrote the story.

Malmolo faboj.

Publication History

"Old Guys With Busted Gaskets" © 2013 Howard Waldrop.

"Why Then Ile Fit You" © 2003 Howard Waldrop. First published in *The Silver Gryphon,* Gary Turner & Marty Halpern, eds.

"The Wolf-man of Alcatraz" © 2004 Howard Waldrop and SCIFI.COM. First published in SCIFICTION.

"The Horse of a Different Color (That You Rode in On)" © 2005 by Howard Waldrop and SCIFI.COM. First published in SCIFICTION.

"'The King of Where-I-Go'" © 2005 by Howard Waldrop and SCIFI.COM. First published in SCIFICTION.

"The Bravest Girl I Ever Knew . . ." © 2005 by Howard Waldrop. First published in *Kong Unbound,* Karen Haber, ed.

"Thin, On the Ground" © 2006 by Howard Waldrop. First published in *Cross Plains Universe,* Scott Cupp and Joe Lansdale, eds.

"Kindermarchen" © 2007 by Howard Waldrop. First published in *Sentinel Science Fiction.*

"Avast, Abaft!" © 2008 by Howard Waldrop. First published in *Fast Ships, Black Sails,* Jeff & Ann VanderMeer, eds.

"Frogskin Cap" © 2009 by Howard Waldrop. First published in *Songs of the Dying Earth,* Gardner Dozois & George R. R. Martin, eds.

"Ninieslando" © 2010 by Howard Waldrop. First published in *Warriors,* Gardner Dozois & George R. R. Martin, eds.

Afterwords © 2013 Howard Waldrop.

About the Author

Howard Waldrop, born in Mississippi and now living in Austin, Texas, is an American iconoclast. His books include *Them Bones* and *A Dozen Tough Jobs,* and the collections *Howard Who?, All About Strange Monsters of the Recent Past, Night of the Cooters* (Locus Award winner), *Other Worlds, Better Lives,* and *Things Will Never Be the Same.* He won the Nebula and World Fantasy Awards for his novelette "The Ugly Chickens."